Minimum of Two

Tim Winton was born in Perth in 1960 and has written novels, collections of stories, non-fiction and books for children. He has won the Miles Franklin Award four times, and been twice shortlisted for the Booker Prize, for *The Riders* (1995) and *Dirt Music* (2002).

Also by Tim Winton

Novels

An Open Swimmer

Shallows

That Eye, The Sky

In the Winter Dark

Cloudstreet

The Riders

Dirt Music

Breath

Stories

Scission

The Turning

Minimum of Two

Tim Winton

PICADOR

First published 1987 by McPhee Gribble Publishers Pty Ltd, Victoria, Australia,
in association with Penguin Books Australia Ltd,
with the assistance of the Literature Board of the Australia Council

First published in Great Britain 1993 by Picador as part of *Blood and Water*

This edition published 2003 by Picador
an imprint of Pan Macmillan Ltd
Pan Macmillan, 20 New Wharf Road, London N1 9RR
Basingstoke and Oxford
Associated companies throughout the world
www.panmacmillan.com

ISBN 978-0-330-41262-9

9 8 7 6 5 4 3 2

A CIP catalogue record for this book is available from
the British Library.

Typeset by SX Composing DTP, Rayleigh, Essex
Printed in the UK by CPI Mackays, Chatham ME5 8TD

Visit **www.picador.com** to read more about all our books
and to buy them. You will also find features, author interviews and
news of any author events, and you can sign up for e-newsletters
so that you're always first to hear about our new releases.

these belong to Jesse and Denise:

my blood, my water

Acknowledgements

A number of these stories have appeared before, in *Island*, *Bulletin*, *MJ*, *Australian Literary Magazine*, *This Australia*, *Matilda*, *Sydney Morning Herald*, *Meanjin*, *Follow Me*, and *Scripsi*; the author thanks these publications.

One and one make one
and one
and one and one make one . . .

Playground chant

Contents

Forest winter

Each day the young man left his wife and child asleep and went out into the forest to saw wood. Winter had closed in. The sawing was bitter work, but it had come at the final moment, before they gave up on the country and went back north to the city and the hardship of the dole. He drove out in the boss's utility and searched for fallen timber which he would cut into blocks and cart back to the tiny valley to store for the holiday season. The bawl of the saw hurt his ears so that at the end of a day's work his head had the same stuffed feel as it had after a night's playing with the band, before everything fell apart.

At noon he sheltered in the utility and ate his lunch of bread and cheese with the rain trickling down the windows and the quiet of the forest coming upon him. It was lonely in the middle of the day with no company but the pale trunks of karri trees. During his morning break, the circumstances of the past few months rested hard on him. When the light was weak and if the wind was especially hard and cold, he would sit, chewing, motionless, almost catatonic from misery. But when it came time to take up the chainsaw again and sharpen its teeth before going back to whichever great, dead tree he was dismembering, he knew with certainty that he was still all right, and the fact that he could swill his tea dregs into the bracken and rise from his haunches with the saw was enough for him to know that he wasn't broken. He had been broken once before, years back, when he was still half a boy, and he knew that when you were beaten properly, you didn't get up; you had to wait for some obscure grace to put you together, and there was no guarantee it would come by a second time.

Most days he returned to the crooked little valley before dusk to see the two dozen timber cabins and the shop and the old school and the ruins of the sawmill echoing with the misanthropic calls of magpies. His boss was a retired farmer who'd bought the valley years ago and turned the remains of the logging town into a holiday village for the spring and autumn. Summer and winter were extreme down here and the place deserted but for the owner and his wife and whoever he hired in the off-season.

It was here the young man and his wife and child found themselves the day their money ran out. By then they were just driving without purpose. Too many things had gone against them. The job and the cabin were a sudden mercy.

A month after they arrived, the young man came home one evening to find that the stove and the fire were still unlit. The small house was cold and in darkness and the baby was screaming.

'Rachel?'

He found his wife on the mattress on the floor with the child beside her. When he turned the light on he saw her on her back, mouth wide, struggling to breathe. Her eyes were so big in her face they frightened him. He scrabbled around in the bedclothes. The baby shrieked.

'Where's your Ventolin? Your inhaler, where's your inhaler?'

The young woman was concentrating too hard on getting air to be able to speak. The noise she made in her throat was like the sound of a bough tearing loose in a storm, back and forth, creaking.

He picked the baby up and took the full force of its squall in his ear as he flattened it to his shoulder. He found the inhaler on the floor between tissues and ointments and folded nappies. He felt panic. He brought the inhaler to her mouth with a spare hand, but she pushed it away. That tearing sound faltered for a moment and she managed a single word.

'Old.'

He looked at the cylinder. It was a pressure-pack the size of a bottle cork. He read the expiry date. Months too old; it was likely useless, perhaps dangerous – he didn't know.

'Oh. God.'

He went into the dark kitchen with the baby. Tears and saliva ran down his neck. He wrapped the pink-faced little boy tighter in his blankets and put him in the carry basket. He took the basket out to the car. The sun was well down but the tops of the karris were visible in silhouette and he could still make out the skeleton of the old water tower. For a moment he considered going to the boss for help; it was only a moment.

With the child screaming out in the car, he dressed his wife and wrapped her in blankets and hoisted her up.

The nearest town was twenty-five kilometres east. As the young man drove the old station wagon hard along the narrow road between the bodies of trees and the eyes of feral cats and foxes, he could barely hear the motor over the baby's screams and the pendulous, tearing respiration of his wife.

Everything had changed. How long had it been since they were happy? The music was gone, the money. And Rachel, what had happened to her? Having the baby had muted her. The forceful, funny girl he had married, had suddenly become placid, listless, sickly, as though she'd had the life torn from her as well as the child. He was afraid the breaking of things had let that old helpless panic get back into him.

Winding down the hill towards Bridgetown, he began to sing madly.

> *A frog went walking on a summer's day,*
> *a-hum, a-hum . . .*

Rachel lay against the seat with her head back, eyes wide. He drove hard. He couldn't let this happen. A scream rose in him, like the night the baby was dragged hollow-chested from her.

> *A frog went walking on a summer's day,*
> *He met Miss Mousie on the way, a-hum, a-hum,*
> *A-hum-a-hum-a-hum!*

The pharmacist was still inside the shop – the young man could see him moving about – but the doors were locked and the CLOSED sign was up. The young man bashed on the glass and noticed in the high beam of the idling station wagon how cut and crusted his own fingers had become. The pharmacist ignored him. He beat the glass harder. He shook the door until the burglar alarm set to ringing. Shedding his white coat, the pharmacist came down the aisle between rows of cough medicines and sweets and stuffed toys. The young man saw he was angry.

He thinks I'm a junkie, he thought; he thinks I'm a fuckin' junkie. In the city, a pharmacist might carry a gun at night. But, God, this was the country. He saw the man mouthing words at him.

'Ventolin!' the young man cried back. 'We want some Ventolin. Turn the alarm off, for God's sake! Open the bloody door.' He looked back in the headlights. Oh, Rachel.

The pharmacist stood looking. The young man pointed to the car.

'Asthma, bugger you. She's sick!' His fists rested on the glass and he was stiff.

The door opened a crack. The alarm rang on. It rang in his head, right through him.

'My wife's got asthma. She can't breathe. She needs Ventolin.'

'Doesn't she carry it?' The pharmacist was tall. He squinted. The young man realized the man couldn't see with the car lights in his eyes.

'It's expired. Look, she's nearly had it.'

'You need a prescription. And money.'

'We've got a nine-week-old baby boy in the back. Or how 'bout my index finger as a deposit. Will that do? For Chrissake!'

'Stay there.'

'Oh, listen to it.'

When the man came back with the tiny cylinder, the young man snatched it from him and ran to the car. Rachel had begun to sob. It was pitiful. He stuck the inhaler between her lips and sprayed it. The bitter smell seeped out. The baby whimpered hoarsely. He sprayed, catching her on the intake. And again. He sank against the seat with the lights on and the motor still running. He saw the pharmacist locking up. The alarm died.

Late in the evening the young man sat in the darkness and drank the coarse volatile claret the locals called Kirup Syrup. The stuff found a big emptiness in him. Relief had consumed something inside. Mother and child were asleep on the mattress in the bedroom. He was weary. There was a day's work ahead in the morning. He could not sleep. Kirup Syrup puckered his mouth and made his lips fatten. After midnight he reeled out into the still forest night and saw clouds rushing across the moon above the crown-shadows of the trees. It was an eerie sight; not a flurry where he stood, but up there a maelstrom. He was grateful for the sight of it. He was thankful for Rachel and the baby. They were something to check himself against. And now he was drunk and would have fallen down asleep in leaf litter if the cold hadn't driven him into bed.

Before dawn, he woke and crept about in an unaccountably cheerful mood. He drank steel-cold water and washed his face and looked at his hands in the half-light. They no longer looked like a guitarist's hands and the fact was suddenly of no consequence. For a while he stood at the bathroom window and watched light and mist and birds moving at the feet of karris where bracken and grasses hung sluggish with dew. Then he went to the bedroom where

Rachel and the baby were stirring. He took the old kerosene tin they used as a wastepaper bin to the kitchen.

At the stove, he tipped the contents of the tin into the firebox. The papers were old bills and envelopes, Kleenex, and a few crumpled sheets that were his latest clumsy attempts at songwriting. He laid some kindling on top and lit it. He went out for more wood.

When he opened the firebox again a few minutes later, the blaze exploded in his face with the sound of a gunshot. He squealed. In that instant his vision was gone, and he fell back against the rickety deal table.

'Jerra? Jerra! What's wrong? What's happened?' He felt her propping him up.

'I can't see,' he cried. 'Nothing.' His eyes felt scorched. There was soot and charcoal grit in his mouth.

'Let me see.'

'Oh, Jesus.'

'Get up.'

'I—'

'Get the hell up, Jerra. Come to the sink.'

He felt her pinching grip on his forearms. Water was splashed on him. For a moment he saw those clouds rushing across the sky; he felt delirious. Somewhere, the baby burbled. He was happy, he felt crazy.

Then there was light. Water in his eyes.

'Better?'

'I dunno.'

'Don't be wet, is it better or not?'

'Yes.' He saw the fogged outline of her arm, and for a moment, a clear vision of her brown eyes. He listened to her wheeze. In a few minutes he could see properly, though his eyes felt as though they were full of ballast.

The kitchen wall was black with soot, and as far back as the opposite wall, pieces of kindling and charcoal were strewn about.

'What was it?'

Rachel straightened from the firebox of the stove and held up the distorted remains of the old Ventolin cylinder. She showed him the metal fragments all over the linoleum.

'Must have tossed it in with the wastepaper,' he said.

'You could have lost your eyes, Jerra.'

'I'll be more careful.'

Out on the back stoop after breakfast, the young man watched the rain coming in from the south. He heard Rachel coughing as she sang to the child.

A frog went walking on a summer's day, a-hum . . .

He sharpened the teeth of the chainsaw and prepared to go out into the day.

No memory comes

1

The boy leaves his parents on the beach and wanders up
through the dunes. Night has fallen and the lights of holiday
shacks are budding on the hill. There is no wind. He hears a
voice, slows down, homes in on it, and falls to his belly at
the vegetated lip of a razorback dune. Down in the bowl
between hills he sees two bodies. Hears them whispering.
The sand on the declivity is fine and wind-smooth. As he
shifts, a tiny ripple begins. He moves back. Another swell
rolls down.

A shout!

The boy sees a man's body rising against the luminous
sand, pulling up his pants. The boy turns and surfs back
down the face of the incline with the sound of a silhouette
behind him. He fights his way through the white seas, up
slope, down-trough, from shadow to light, until he comes
out on the flat beach where his mother and father sit talking
low and he sees no one behind.

Happy New Year, his mother says.

Happy New Year, his father says.

A year has passed. He is older. He does not believe it.

That night he climbs into bed between his parents. His father muffles a weedy fart. His mother sleeps with a glick in her throat. The boy worms in and gets ready to dream that the new year will never come. Everything is fine right now. He has no need of it.

2

The boy is in love with school. He knows he is young. He knows he doesn't need to fly to Hong Kong every week or wash clothes. He only has to go to school and say things right and try hard. He only has to see his friends and not get caught playing British Bulldog.

On the way home he walks with a boy from a Catholic school. They both live on the hill behind the beach. In the summer they are in the same swimming classes – their patter kick and their duck dives are about the same. By the end of the summer they are best friends. Summers go by, but the boy knows everything stays the same. Even at twelve he doesn't feel any older.

At the end of one summer, the boy and his friend, on their way to the beach, find a man dead in his car. There is a hose from the exhaust going into the boot. It takes them a long time to decide the man is not asleep. When the ambulance comes and the men break the windows to pull the man out, the boys see the upholstery look of the dead man's face. When the ambulance leaves, the boy's friend begins to cry. He tells the boy that he wets the bed every night. And once his father tied the wet pyjamas round his neck and sent him to the Catholic school like that. This is his biggest secret. The boy sits on the kerb and watches his friend's fists. In the vacant lot behind, the wind stirs the whispering wild oats.

Later that week, the boy visits his friend's place and pisses in his father's golf buggy. He is older now, he knows, but he knows too that he and his friend will never change.

3

The boy goes to high school. He likes it after a while, though it is never as good as primary school. His friend leaves the Catholic school and they are in the same classes.

The boy still has weekends up the coast with his parents in the little asbestos house. His father drinks beer and his mother reads.

After school the boy and his friend ride down to the beachfront, and if there is no surf they play pinball and pool at the Snakepit and Minderbinders. They see bikies and rockers. The boy knows his mother came from here when she was a widgie. He has never seen a widgie, but he feels it is right that the place should still be there for him.

Sometimes the boy and his friend lie on the sand and talk about where they will hide when the world ends. They talk about God now and then, but it always brings them back to the end of the world. One afternoon, there on the sand with a dollar's worth of chips, they make a vow to look out for each other when it happens. They know it is only a matter of time. The burger joint winks and gulls hang over them and everything is solemn.

4

The boy hears his mother on the phone. When she is finished, she tells him his father is not coming back from Hong Kong because he has fallen in love with the housegirl. She lights a cigarette. He goes into the bathroom, locks the door, turns the shower on full belt, and cries. He beats the tile wall and his knuckles lift.

His mother gets a job. The boy comes home to an empty house. He does his homework, he mucks around with his best friend. He doesn't go up the coast any more, even though his mother got the beach house in the divorce settlement.

The boy looks through old photo albums.

5

The boy bores people at parties. He tells them everything he remembers. He remembers everything. He knows the name of every song on every old record. He knows the name of every member of his first school class. He knows the name of every boy a girl had ever liked. When everyone gets their hair cut and gelled, he keeps his long. His Hawaiian shirt makes people laugh. Girls get drunk and go to sleep in his lap. After every party he waits for his friend, cleans vomit off him, separates him from a clinging girl and they go home together. Everything stays the same between them.

At sixteen they buy a car together. They save by selling milk bars their own empty bottles. They sell their bikes. The boy sells his newest record. They wash cars. They get a paper round. The car is an old HR Holden. They paint it green with brushes and housepaint.

The boy's friend is the first to turn seventeen and get a licence to drive. Together they cruise along the coast and into the city. One night rockers kick the windscreen in at traffic lights. They U-turn into a one-way street. They have to turn around again on the footpath. Back on the beach where it is quiet they buy a bottle of green ginger wine and remember it.

The boy's friend gets a regular girlfriend. The boy doesn't mind. They all ride around together. She graduates from the back seat to the front. After a while the boy finds himself sitting in the back. He doesn't mind. In the back he stretches out and tells old stories. On lonely hills overlooking the river, cruising down neon streets on hot nights, parked beneath the sound of gulls and pinball machines, he tells them how it used to be.

The boy's friend and the girl are voted Head Boy and Head Girl at school. He votes for his friend because they are best mates. He votes for the girl out of loyalty. People say they make a fine couple.

At the school ball the boy gets so drunk his friend makes him go outside and sleep in the car. He wakes to the sound of rocking on the front seat. At the girl's final squeal, his jeans fill with a terrible heat. He swears things are the same.

The boy's friend keeps the car at his own place, even though they both drive now. The boy doesn't mind. His friend still picks him up and he rides in the back and drinks beer and passes out and wakes to a little squeal.

Signs go up all over the beachfront. Redevelopment. High-rise project. Luxury hotel. Observation tower. The boy doesn't believe it will happen. The beach has always been the same. Even for his mother.

Through his bedroom window in the early morning, he is woken by the sound of bulldozers. Someone will stop it; he knows they will.

6

The boy finishes his final-year exams. The year has almost ended. A year no longer feels like a year. Summers seem patchy and short. After the graduation party he rides with his friend and the girl down to the beach where they drink beer from the jagged end of a bottle they open on the door. The burger joints and pinball parlours are gone. Security fences and puce floodlights surround the cranes and the ugly bones of the hotel tower. The boy feels a hole open in him. He strains beer through his teeth.

His friend and the girl flex on the front seat but he can't absent himself. There's a faint, wet breeze, but nothing moves outside. Twisted cartons and stuck-flat wrappers park on the asphalt. The cyclone wire fences glint salty with moisture. Down on the sand, gulls make lumps of themselves in sleep.

In a week he will no longer be a schoolboy. Every morning he wakes with a hard ball of panic in his stomach.

The wet, butcher's-shop sound of lips and tongues. The girl sighs. From the back seat, the boy begins a story about how he once caught so many prawns in the river with his father that they had to take off their clothes and tie knots in the arms and legs and use them as bags to carry prawns that overflowed the tubs. The girl springs up off the seat in front, breasts afloat, and turns the radio on full belt. For a while the boy stays stuck fast in a corner of the back seat. The song makes the whole car vibrate. He feels his eyes itching. He holds his breath.

> *The beach is a place where a man can feel*
> *he's the only soul in the world that's for real . . .*

It's an old record. A mob of things rush him. He remembers. He remembers.

> *And I see a face coming through the haze*
> *I remember him from those crazy days . . .*

People should be born old and die young, he thinks. Grow back; grow back. Memories everywhere.

His friend starts the car. The boy jerks. Next year no one will know them.

They buy more beer. Under the lights of the drive-in bottle shop, the boy remembers the shack up the coast. He remembers sunburn so bad his mother bathed him with vinegar. No beginnings then, and no endings.

From the back seat he tells them about the beach shack. The girl says it's too far and why didn't he remember it before. He shrugs. Thought you were a professional rememberer, she says. They drive up the highway with her laughing. The boy sits in the back trying to catch his friend's eye in the rear-view mirror. He gulps down a can of beer. He sits back with all the windows open and feels the wind take him. Remembers the haze coming down on the beach.

Outside the city, the hot, moist night smells of grass. Backyards, summer. The girl's perfume streaks back to him, triggering. His mother? No, a squeal outside the gym and a flush of heat.

Down a narrow limestone road they wind. Here the dunes are bald and creeping. Sound of heavy surf. The air smells of peppery coastal plants. Black shapes emerge as houses. The boy points out an asbestos place. He opens his third can and pours it scalding-cold down his throat.

With the motor off there is only the sound of the sea. There is no key. The boy gets the jack out of the car and puts it through a window. He doesn't feel drunk. He is starting to feel dead. The girls call him an idiot. His friend sheepishly turns the power on. Inside, everything is carpeted with dust. Walking on the linoleum they leave footprints. Around the walls stand big iron beds, and on shelves, fat paperbacks. A wicker craypot. In the sink drain, the skeleton of a mouse. Out of his deadness, the boy feels panic coming.

They sit on beds. The girl sighs. His friend looks away. The boy looks at his friend's girl. She is slim and brown and her breasts stand up under her singlet top. She has dark, small lips and deep eyes. He asks: Aren't you afraid of getting old? She asks: Is there any beer left? His friend goes out to the car. She sniffs and follows. The boy watches their footprints.

Nothing.

His friend comes back. No beer left. Is he all right? Doesn't he want to go home?

But the boy springs up and begins to hunt for beer. His father kept loads of it. The boy tears cupboards open and guts them, tossing aside bloated tins of pork and ricecream while his friend stands by.

The girl comes inside and asks where is the toilet. The boy points the way and keeps rooting in the cupboards. When she returns, she holds out an old can. A rusty, unopened beer can. The boy takes it. Must be a thousand years old, his friend says. It has no rip-top. It is the kind people used to open with a knife-like opener.

The boy drags a drawer out and finds the old, black opener. It looks like a scythe. You can't drink it, his friend says. But the boy knows he can. There are no memories coming, of course he can.

He slams the flaky old can on to the Laminex table. Braces it against his thigh. Brings the point of the blade to rest on the corroded top. Hard to get a purchase. He leans down hard on the blade. The can slips aside. He feels the cold shock of steel in his groin. He takes in a jet of air. The can rolls across the table and thumps on the floor, keeps rolling.

What? His friend looks at him.

What? the girl says.

The boy looks at the blood on his hand. His friend grabs him and for a moment they hold hands like that, gore slipping between their fingers.

His friend looks down. Oh, shit! Oh!

Laugh, the boy thinks, losing his grip; laugh!

7

Wind tears at him, tearing him down. The motor beats like a heart in his ears. There is heat in his jeans. A warm, warm bath. A year starts to feel like a year again, but no memory comes.

Gravity

Jerra Nilsam sat with his son at a café table and the breeze
was in his shirt. The day was all but gone from him now,
and there was a party to attend. To host, in fact. It was a
friend's birthday. He was late but he was in no hurry. A
party didn't seem to matter a damn today. He felt a little
punch drunk. How could a party count for anything on the
anniversary of your father's death? He wanted to know:
how the hell could anything matter?

This morning he'd woken full of ghostly sensations like
those he'd always associated with amputees. He was afraid.

With great concentration, the little boy made a handprint
with ice cream on the glass table, and looking beyond him,
Nilsam saw the traffic pass. He had come to love the city. It
was no capitulation on his part; merely a gradual awareness
of new beauties. He was older now, he felt it.

'Go home, Daddy?'

'In a minute, mate. Let me finish my coffee.' Wait, little
man, he thought. Let me linger.

Nilsam's pulse quickened, as though he were about to
take a leap.

The three-year-old's eyes were intent on him. They were
black, beneath his fair hair.

'Pongs?'

'No, you can leave your thongs off, if you want. But finish your ice cream.'

The child held the dripping cone out to show he had eaten enough. Nilsam took it, licked it once, and upended it in the ashtray.

'OK. Come on, me mate.' His throat felt tight and he heard his heart working hard.

Through the flat streets they rode with the wind in their faces. The boy sat strapped into his seat over the rear wheel with his rubber thongs threaded up his forearms. He shrilled a song Rachel would sing him in the bath in the mornings, the quiet time when Nilsam transcribed with an ear to the sounds of the house.

'Green for go!' cried the boy, beating him on the back.

Nilsam coasted through the lights. Heat. Sweat. Pulse.

'Ready for the party?' he yelled back over his shoulder. The boy clapped. Oh, God, the party.

'Yaaa!'

They rattled past parked cars to beat the sunset home.

Their street was always full of cars, but now there were so many there didn't seem to be enough room for houses. As they coasted into the driveway, Jerra heard the music. It was his own music they were playing, his not very famous songs. His heart contracted.

'Party!' the boy cried. 'Yaay!'

Nilsam got off and wheeled the bike up the leafy side of the house. He had to struggle to counterbalance the child's excited lurching. The sudden light and roar of the packed yard stopped him dead. People, some friends, greeted him. They tickled the boy. He smelt the thin, cutting edge of tobacco smoke and the subtlest hint of dope. Everywhere was light, in jewellery and bottles and eyes and glasses. Food passed him. He saw how trodden the lawn was. He was glad to see the door to his studio padlocked. It was an old shed his father had renovated for him. Rachel turned from where she stood speaking with friends across the courtyard and saw him. He knew there was trouble.

'Juice? Drink, Daddy?' the little boy shrilled. 'Loud.' He covered his ears. 'Loud.'

Nilsam leant the bicycle against the paling fence, unstrapped the child and led him to a table where he let him pour himself a drink. Lemonade sloshed on to the hired tablecloth. The boy smiled around the glass.

'Good?' Nilsam asked. His mouth was dry and a heaviness was in him.

'Marvellous.'

'Where'd you get a word like that?' But the child was drinking again and the bubbles made him giggle.

He felt Rachel at his side. She was tall and slim. Her dark hair was out and she wore a cotton dress. Her tan made her look as though she was made from polished jarrah. He was sad.

'Where were you, for God's sake? I thought you must have had an accident.'

'We stayed too long at the Italia. It was cool, wasn't it, Sam? Sorry.' He thought he could smell suntan oil. It was the frangipani in bloom.

'You haven't done a bloody thing for this. Poor Ann thinks you've snubbed her. Philip is drunk—'

'OK.' She was beginning to cry, it always frightened him. 'What do you want me to do?'

'Oh, Jerra.'

Rachel went inside and left him with the heavy scent of

the frangipani and a strange, hurtling sensation. His music jangled out at him. He went across, under the pergola, to the tapedeck, cut the music, pulled out the tape and put something else in, something fashionable.

Philip intercepted him on his way to the back door.

'Modesty strikes him down.' Philip pointed at the cassette in Nilsam's hand.

'Hi, Phil.'

'My wife is offended.'

'And you're drunk. I've heard.'

Philip had got thin these past years. Eight years back he'd married Ann and they'd honeymooned in Nilsam's shack on the south coast, though it had not been a success. Ann had grown fat. Nilsam carried too much weight himself and it had begun to annoy him. Philip looked pasty. His soft, hairless face had the practised vulnerability of the social worker. Nilsam liked him, but not tonight.

'Tell her I'm sorry, eh?' Jerra said. He touched Philip on the arm as was expected. 'And tell her she's a silly bitch for getting offended.'

He left Philip with a cheap hurt look on his face and went inside. People fussed in the kitchen. In the laundry, someone broke ice with a hammer. He heard the tail end of a joke. Seats in the living room were pulled into pairs. Social workers, he thought; more bloody Deep and Meaningfuls. It's a party, for God's sake.

Rachel was in the bedroom. She sat in the big, ugly reading chair with a biography of Thomas Merton across her bare knee. He knew she hadn't been reading.

'You've ruined it.'

'I know.' He saw the mahogany sheen of her folded leg.

'What's the matter with you?'

'I don't know.' He couldn't bring himself to mention his father. *You should know!* he wanted to bellow. 'I really am sorry.'

Her mouth closed against him. When she did that he could see her age. He picked up a little orange gumboot from the floor.

'He insists on wearing these bloody things all summer,' he said with a weak laugh.

'Where *is* Sam?'

'I don't know. Out the back somewhere. Probably scoffing the horses' doovers. He'll stink of anchovies tonight. I'll have to sleep in the spare room. Come on. We better go outside and be hosts.'

But out under the party lights of the pergola, his new resolve waned. His smile split his face, his jokes petered out mid-sentence; he couldn't look their friends in the eye. Ann stood with two other women beside a table bristling with bottles. He caught her looking at him, looked away.

You're thirty years old, he told himself; be adult enough to go and smooth things over. He got himself a glass of Semillon. He took a few serious breaths. And he stayed where he was. He stood rigid beside Rachel as she spoke with their guests.

There was a hole in him. Something was lost. The tall man in loose grey trousers with that stooped, expectant stance. The big hands so often hairy with pollard. Only a memory now. He was dead. Actually, finally, dead. And now there was nothing for Jerra Nilsam to fall against. He thought about the ride home. His heart beating. It was riding down that street, as though he had been balancing a bicycle for the first time. There was no exhilaration in it, only a terrible sense of gravity.

The party wore on. Bottles emptied and the lawn was flattened with sporadic dancing until, in the middle of it all, someone gagged the stereo and brought out a guitar. A thin droopy young man began to play 'Stairway to Heaven'. Nilsam groaned. Dancers bitched quietly beneath the frangipani.

'It's 1985, for God's sake,' he muttered. '1973 is over.' Someone shushed him. Someone else tittered.

'Amateurs not good enough for you?' a woman hissed from across the courtyard.

Nilsam found a chair at the end of the garden. He'd wait it out. From there he overheard the same conversations about IVF, family therapy, AIDS. After a while, Sam came by, slit-eyed and cranky. He put the child over his knee and put him to sleep with 3/4 time pats on the back.

Nilsam weathered it out, protected from conversation by the sleeping child.

'Use the brakes, Jerra!' Old man running behind. Tinsel on the lawn. Christmas. Old man holding the back of the seat. Charging around the yard on the reddest bike in the world. And then the grip gone, no old man. Sudden grave feeling of independence. Turning, turning. 'You'll be right!' the old man calls. Then the roses, the thorns, looming. Whooaa!

He woke with a flinch. Craziness in his belly, as though he was about to fall. He put his face to the little boy's neck and closed his eyes.

Neither Rachel nor Ann spoke to him when he helped them clean up. He collected bottles and broken glasses, picked up cigarette butts with dramatic disdain, swept, sighed. When they went inside he knew better than to join them. Philip was asleep in a deckchair, face disfigured by snoring. Nilsam unlocked the studio behind the courtyard, went in and shut the door.

The studio was foetid and dusty. Egg cartons on the walls gave it a spooky look. There was little room in which to move; the place was full of microphones on stands, cords, a piano, an organ, various guitars, mandolin, metronome, sheets of paper, bits of carpet and blanket and rickety chairs. Here Nilsam wrote songs and sold them to singers who never quite sang them well enough or in the presence of people influential enough to make him rich. They were not love songs and not particularly sad. Rachel sang them to Sam at bedtime and bathtime, and having her sing them was enough for him to continue. But she never sang in front of him. He had to eavesdrop to hear her husky, wavery voice. The sound of it made his skin prickle the way it had the first day he saw her on Scarborough Beach. It had been autumn and he had come back to the city with his mind cooled enough to set a little and see the shape of things and bear it.

He turned the eight-track on. He listened for a few moments to his doodlings on a keyboard and then he switched it off. For a long time, he did nothing but sit in the haven the old man had built for him. It was his father's idea to build it before the cancer beat him down and his blood turned to water. He knew his son was no handyman. It was something between them, like the old days. The old man said it was his Ark. Rachel teased the old man and called it the Tower of Babel. He built it anyway and at the end of summer he died.

When Nilsam went out into the warm night, Philip was gone from the deckchair and the house was in darkness.

Sam and Rachel were asleep. He slid into bed beside them. He lay a while, listening to their sounds, and the old melancholy took him. He lifted the blind a little so he could see them in the light from the street. Rachel's hair was plaited and thick on the pillow. Sam was face-down between the pillows, looking – as always – as though he'd fallen asleep crawling, and in a moment he saw the birth again, the awful rending of flesh, the tiny blue slug tossed on to Rachel's belly, the crew snatching him away to work on that sunken little chest, that hiccuping little chest, and letting go the blind, he fell back on his pillow.

Rachel and Sam slept on, and in time Jerra was left limp, and his mind was clear.

In that dim room with its smells of talcum and incense and anchovy breath, Jerra remembered how he and Rachel took him to the old man's bedside, the last time when the toddler smiled and quivered and the old man drank him up, his flesh, his scent, his life. 'Blood,' the old man said. It was his joke.

Nilsam was a father. He was a husband. He was a son.

Cars rattled past on the street outside. The Bulgarian's dog was barking again. Nilsam pulled Sam to him. He slipped an arm under him and cupped the little buttocks in their pyjamas.

Rachel turned with a sigh. He lifted the blind again. The faint light showed him her face. It was so familiar it might have been his own. He felt her breath on him. The house creaked. He knew where he was. The Bulgarian's dog barked. A Volkswagen pulled in next door. He even knew the time by that; it was four o'clock. A rooster crowed. Something receded in him.

At dawn he took Sam in his arms out to the toilet. The grass was cold. Sam pissed on the seat. The homely ammoniac smell made Nilsam grin. He hoisted the sleeping

25

boy on to his shoulder and took him across the dewy lawn towards the house. Sun moved across the rooftops. A phrase of music came to him, something fresh which made his heart tic. This afternoon he would go and see his mother. Today he would do many things. He took the boy inside, put him in bed beside Rachel and climbed in. Sleep came to him and he was not afraid.

The water was dark and it went forever down

The girl left her mother in the rented cottage with all the shades drawn and went down to the packed white sand of the beach. She passed the jetty with its whirling braid of gulls and followed the line of the bay. She was tall for her age, but years of training in the pool had taken lankiness from her. Her hair was cropped close. In the summer sun her big nose had gone scabby. She just wished her mother would put the bottles away, raise the blinds, and come outside into the world again, but the girl knew she had a better chance of making the Olympics than changing her mother.

Eight years ago, when the girl was six years old and her father had been gone a year, her mother had a terrible accident. Depressed and drunk, she passed out while smoking in bed and woke in flames. Her nylon nightie crackled and hissed. She beat herself out on the floor and threw a jug of water over the bed, but she did not call out to the girl across the hall. She sat shaking in the dark with a bottle of sherry until dawn when she phoned an ambulance. Because she waited, her scars were hideous. Years later, she told the girl she hadn't wanted to alarm her by shrieking and waking her in the middle of the night looking the way she did, like a charred side of beef. From that moment the girl was convinced that her mother was either stupid or sick.

Down the front of her bikini, the girl saw her tiny breasts and was grateful that her own body was unblemished. Even these days, the sight of her mother caused her teeth to clench. She kicked up a string of kelp and watched it settle back on the sand. This holiday was so boring. There was no one her age. Already she'd run out of books. It was no different from home.

Following the curve of the bay, she saw the small island offshore – low, rocky, spotted with vegetation – and she wondered how far out it was.

She knew her mother was sick and bitter and afraid. She just wished she could pull herself out of it, get a job, stay out of mental hospitals, save for some special surgery, find a man. God, to be *normal*!

All those stupid, recurring statements ran through her head. *'All a person needs is a bit of land,'* her mother would say, *'that's what makes the difference.'* *'Men hate us. They hate our bodies.'* *'God has been cruel to me.'* *'Your father never loved you.'* These came up during TV programmes, at meals; the girl heard them shouted in the night, heard them screeched from their sixth-floor window as she slunk home from training. Over and over.

A hot breeze blew off the land, from where the colossal white backs of dunes humped at the edge of town, threatening the place with their shifting weight.

She's gonna send me crazy, she thought.

Every night after school, the girl trained in the swimming squad. It was three hours of blind, busting effort, away from home, and though she didn't love it the way the others did, she knew she couldn't be without it.

The girl stopped walking. It was stupid to walk, she knew. Walking made you think. What she needed was a swim; to be an engine.

By now the island was directly out from her. Crayboats passed it, their motors coming from weird directions in the wind.

An old man on a sailboard skimmed past with a ludicrous smile on his face. With a grunt, she ran to the water and speared into the channel and swam.

She had good style. Her breathing was metrical. She was tuned for it. She swam and thought the thoughts of a machine.

Out in the centre of the channel the water was dark and it went forever down. The island seemed no closer.

She moved all her parts. Everything did its task. She was not tired.

When the water suddenly became warmer, she knew she was there. Standing in the shallows, just out from a little sandy beach, she saw a cloud of birds and heard the blood chug in her ears.

'All a person needs is a bit of land,' she said aloud. She laughed and it wasn't all derision.

She stretched her arms. She noticed that she'd left her watch on. It had stopped. She guessed the swim had taken her fifteen minutes. The easterly was drying her already, leaving streaks of salt on her flesh.

The island was a bird sanctuary. There were signs and warnings. It wasn't a big island. Maybe ten hectares she guessed, or less. She climbed up from the beach and wandered across the island's humpbacked plateau. Seabirds

filled the sky; they nested in holes in the ground and limestone nooks; they chased each other in territorial battles and
shrieked from places unseen. On the packed sand, scrub
and limestone monoliths offered little shelter. The tracks
of birds peppered every soft surface. The whole place smelt
birdy. On the seaward side surf creased across reefs, and
small, sunken lagoons and potholes stood still and full.
From the low cliffs she could see fish down in the water with
birds diving on them. Underfoot, wherever she went, broken
eggshells mashed and blew. As she walked, a murmur grew
and birds fled before her. One ran blindly from its hole and
skidded off her shin. Thousands, thousands of black birds.

In their midst, in the centre of the island, the girl sat
down to watch them soar and stitch about her. She wondered why they thrived so. She thought of Biol. class and
tried to think. There seemed to be plenty of fish for them to
eat. No predators that she could see – no sign of snakes.
Just birds, and she didn't even know what kind. Hatch-
ing, growing, hunting, mating, dying. There was something
relentlessly single-minded about the whole business.

After a time, she stood up and more birds rose with her,
taking their atonal music with them. By her foot, she saw the
carcass of a small bird. All over the island she found dead
birds: whole, mutilated, broken. And shells and feathers.
And shit. A constant layer of debris. She felt within the grasp
of something important, something she might understand.
From Biol. What did that skinny teacher with the tobacco
breath call it? That was it – the web of life. She saw it all
before her. The sick and the weak died and the young
and the strong lived and thrived. It's the way things are, she
thought. You need to just *go*, that was it; survive, win.

All you need is a bit of land . . . something solid under

you. Ah, what rubbish, especially from her mother. Something solid, and there she was all day in the dark, drinking. A life of fluids. A whole ocean she must have drunk by now and she talked about *land*! Bird sanctuary for a lame duck. She was tired of fighting it all, always always swimming over the top of that sea of grog. Maybe that's why I started swimming, she thought, to stop her drowning me.

She went back down to the sandy beach and she took off her watch and bikini and lay in the sun. Her body was strong and hard. She was young. There was no more room, she decided, for feeling sorry for dead things and dying things and sick things; for her mother or even herself. Now there was only time to live, to survive. Live. Survive. They're the same thing, she told herself quickly. No difference.

She got up and saw that she had left her perfect shape in the sand, and then she cried out in triumph and ran naked down to the water and pierced it and began to swim.

Be an engine. Don't complain. Don't ask. Don't hesitate. Swim, don't think.

Pushing out, she knew that as soon as she was old enough she would leave her mother. There was no room. She had to look after herself, leave her mother to the web. There wasn't time enough any more for all this swimming through craziness and ugliness and dumbness, sherry, beer, Scotch, gin.

Be an engine.

But she faltered.

Don't think, breathe!

She moved her parts. Swimming machine.

Think.

No, you old bitch. I can swim.

She cut through the water and filled up cold with anger and went harder.

I can be a machine. Like a fish, you old bitch. I can swim away.

Harder.

Go.

Do.

Cut.

Harder.

That body thrashed and whitened the water, throttling out, vibrating, parts shearing away, roaring white hot, and all the way down she felt young and strong and perfect in the cold darkness.

Nilsam's friend

for Galloway and Chambers

Looking up from the page Nilsam saw his friend come up the path, distorted in the gentle convexities of the leadlight window. He stood and the chair crashed into the wall. The window shrieked as he opened it.

'Well, butter my bread,' Nilsam said with his head stuck out.

His friend looked up with a grin. His hair was thick and his beard was long and lustrous in the creamy sunlight. He was thin and barefoot as usual, but hair and beard formed such a magnificent mane that it made him seem bigger, thicker.

'You look like a lion.'

Nilsam's friend stopped below the window. The air was congested with the sounds of birds and cicadas. A dog barked. It was spring in Perth. Nilsam's friend wore the tiger-striped calico pants his girlfriend had made, and a black T-shirt bearing the words SURFERS AGAINST NUCLEAR DESTRUCTION. He squinted in the sun.

'Got in last night.'

'You're early.'

'Ran out of money in Athens.'

Nilsam shook his head. 'Athens.'

Both of them broke into laughter.

Nilsam left the window and went through the house to the front door. It was cool in here. The dark boards croaked as he went. So the old romantic is back, he thought; the perpetual adolescent. He wondered for how long. Nilsam's friend could not decide whether or not to marry. He embarked on trips to 'get his head together' but a decision was never forthcoming. There were always stories; he brought back atmosphere by the suitcase, but never a solution to his dilemma. At least this time he looks well, Nilsam thought. Last time he looked like something out of Belsen.

'The boy asleep?' Nilsam's friend asked as they embraced at the door.

'Yeah.'

'I bet he's twice the size.'

'He's learnt to say shit.'

'I turned thirty in a monastery.'

'Good grief, let's get some food and go out into the sun.'

In the kitchen, Nilsam pulled the cork from a bottle of wine and he gave his friend a salami and a cheese with a little knife in it.

'Thirty.'

They sat out on the back lawn which was strewn with bright plastic toys. They ate and drank. Nilsam's friend looked hard and wiry. His eyes looked good and clear. He told Nilsam stories about the crazy Greek peasants living in the old church, about the lump on his girlfriend's breast they'd flown to London to have removed; about the airlessness of the English; about Greece again and the tavernas and the white light and the donkeys; about the surf in Spain and the ecumenical monastery in France where he'd arrived sick and been taken into the infirmary like a medieval pilgrim; about the icons; about things that happened to him that he couldn't explain properly, and Nilsam listened and felt overweight, sluggish, ignorant and still a little disdainful. He was working. He had a son to look after, and a wife to consider. He didn't have time for romantic jaunts. He didn't have the money or the hide. And, dammit, he didn't want to go.

'I wished you were there, sometimes, you and Rachel and the Terror.'

'We'd have slowed you down,' Nilsam said. He poured some more wine. It was thick and red against the liverish grass.

'Well, I missed you all like hell anyway. Greece, mate, you'd love it.'

'Greece? I've got most of it in this neighbourhood.'

'But the retsina, the tavernas, the light, the colour of the ocean.'

'People say the light, the sea, the . . . well, it's the same as here.'

'It doesn't matter. Yeah, it's a lot like here. But it's not here.'

Nilsam shrugged. It always came to this.

The back door opened. Nilsam's son, rumpled and squinty from sleep, toddled out into the sun and fell into his lap.

'He *has* grown.'

'He's crapped himself, too,' Nilsam said with a smile, and he put his lips to the child's hay-smelling hair.

'You're good with him.'

Nilsam shrugged. He felt dowdy. He was a man and he felt dowdy like women were supposed to feel dowdy.

'Did you see the rooster?' He pointed up the back.

'What's it, a leghorn–emu cross?'

'Biggest rooster in the world.'

Nilsam's friend laughed.

'Reminds me,' Nilsam said. 'A little girl bumped into me coming out of a record shop yesterday while I was riding past. She must have been eight or so and she'd dropped her Bach record. I asked her about it. She looked at me and said: "Bach was the greatest composer in the world. So was Handel." I had to ride a whole block before I could laugh without a conscience. Nearly fell off me bike.'

The child rolled over in his lap and reached for the knife on the grass.

'Ta? Ta?'

'No, not for boys.'

The child turned over and began to cry.

'I'm winding down,' Nilsam's friend said. 'Got in at four this morning.'

'Go home and get some sleep,' Nilsam said, grappling with the child.

'Yeah.'

They walked through the house to the front door and on the veranda they stood in the noonday shade and looked out across the suburb with its close-set houses and smudges of smoke from the spring burn-off.

'By the way,' Nilsam said, 'what's the verdict?'

'I turned thirty. It put me out of kilter. Couldn't decide.'

Nilsam smiled and his friend went down the steps.

In the afternoon he sat out there as the sun ate into the shade. He watched his son climb the steps with fierce concentration as he waited for his wife to get home from work, and he caught himself wondering what it was like to see the same creamy light, the same blue eye of the ocean, the same sky-colours somewhere else.

Minimum of two

I felt Greta in the dark and her buttocks were cool as honey-dew. She stirred. Her breasts came my way and puckered against my face. I hoped to God she would stay asleep. I ached with my own blood. Gently, I squared her hips to me, displaced a bent knee and settled in between her legs. Her fine hair fell across my mouth. She breathed her sweet melon smell. I felt the curve of jaw, line of neck, heard the satin whisper of a shifting thigh and all the caution went out of me as I pushed her back, writhed up into her, levering on my toes until I prised her open. She gave a little cry. Her knees locked me at the hips. I scrambled and shunted with my head blank. Greta, my wife, began to scream. Her nails lifted buds of flesh from my back. She headbutted me and I yawed off her, spilling across the bed into the cold. There was a small silence before a car started up across the street and Greta began to make broken noises that might have been retching or weeping, though I couldn't tell because I got the hell out.

Among the sawdust drifts in my workshop, I threw tools at the wall and kicked drums, lurching in a sweat from one end to the other until I could barely breathe any more and I fell in a corner against an old chest full of bolts and brackets.

The fluorescent light made me feel puny. I was still naked. I smelt of Greta. I was ashamed. That hatred came back and I got frightened of myself.

I thought of that bastard Blakey cornering her in the dungeon-shadows of the car park, and of the features of her face collapsing as she backed against a fender, then a pillar, then a wall. The things he did to her, those details that everyone heard at the trial, the things he said, the things I listened to her say in a dead tone. I thought of her quiet on the piss-smelling concrete and her blood on his business suit; now in my mind I couldn't stop from seeing her pulling her clothes together as he showed her to her car and strapped her in and sent her on her way to be on her best behaviour. The look of her when she came into the house that night nearly three years ago made me want to die.

She was like a ghost for two weeks. I couldn't get a word out of her but I heard her crying in the bathroom at night. When I found the bruises on her I forced it out of her. I took her to the police. A week or so after that, she thawed a little and I knew she was coping. Her big laugh came back and the softness in her eyes. There was a rash on her chest sometimes that came and went but she seemed OK. After my first rage I put it all to the back of my mind. I told myself that what was important was getting Greta back into herself. I wanted to give her all the time she needed.

It was some time before she could be touched, but she softened up. We stayed home, felt intimate again. I was frightened to even suggest sex, but it was her idea in the end. We decided to have a baby. Big and round and rich, Greta never looked better. Seeing her pregnant made me happy and I knew it was all right with us again.

Blakey was Greta's senior in the Department. She took

too long to act. The jury procrastinated as though maybe the whole thing was Greta's fault, but Blakey got five years with a minimum before parole of two. We sat like wood in the courtroom, Greta and me. The lawyer was smug. There were photographers. They begged us to smile.

After the trial, I stopped work for a few weeks. The house was quiet. Greta went back to what she was like the months after it first happened; it was like a relapse. She cried a lot, moved potted plants from place to place around the house, smoked three packs a day, had nightmares, wouldn't talk about it. A few weeks passed. I took her out for a game of tennis; she wore a tracksuit even though there was sun. We drove up into the hills. Had big dinners at home and got drunk and slept well. I'd worked hard on the house ever since the first night she came home like a ghost and now it was good to be in. Winter was coming. Greta stayed around the house. Because it was cosy, she said. I knew I was helping.

She got better. The twins were born and she cried for three days, but she pulled herself together. I worked hard and brought in a lot of money and improved the house still more. Everything was good. Greta was content with the boys.

But something went wrong somewhere. Six months after the twins were born, Greta changed. She seemed distracted. She was a scrupulous mother, she did everything right, she spared the twins nothing, but I'd come into the room and find her suckling them, one on each breast, with a look of awful sadness on her face. She looked as though she was waiting to die.

Not long after, she stopped eating meat. It didn't bother me. When I saw it made her ill to see me eat it, I quit too.

The kids grew. I climbed into work each morning, and

for eight hours I thought of nothing but the smell and the feel and the weight of wood. I made us a lot of money.

For a long time Greta hid the rash from me. It was red and ugly and puckered. Her skin felt as though it had been embossed. Greta said it was a side-effect of the pill.

We didn't linger over sex. It was a gradual thing. Greta never joked about it any more. I started going without. It was weeks, then months. The boys took my mind off it. I used to laugh at their crazy infant dialect as we played under the big purple lilac in the spring.

I waited for her – she was my wife – I knew she needed time. But there was nothing. Even Greta's affection for me seemed to dry up. She never touched me, never said anything gentle; there was no intimacy in her. She hardly looked at me. Every now and then she would get drunk and melt a little, enough to laugh and to hug me and even lead me to the bedroom, but it always ended with her in tears and me going mad out in the workshop.

It was like starving to death.

Greta saw doctors about the rash. She saw a psychotherapist about sex but he wanted her dreams and I could have told him that Greta never remembered dreams.

Some nights when I fled to the workshop, her weeping sounded wrong. I thought I heard laughter. It was a sick noise. My whole life was warping like a plank in the sun. That's when the hatred came into me.

The night I was desperate and pitiful enough to try to make love with my wife while she was asleep, the night that made her look at me as though I was diseased, that was the night I decided to kill Fred Blakey.

*

41

When I went back inside that night, the house was quiet. I went to the big grey filing cabinet in the study and took out all our documents relating to the trial: letters from the lawyer, copies of legal documents, some rape pamphlets, a few notes I'd made during the proceedings. I sifted them on the desk. It made me cold to see the letterheads, even the shape of my own handwriting from the time. In the file there was a slip of paper which bore nothing but the words: a minimum of two. Blakey might be out already, I thought. I checked back through the dates. No, he'd still be inside, but nearly due for parole. The twins found me asleep in the reading chair in the morning. They thought it was great fun.

During the day I looked up some old telephone directories and found where Blakey's house was and at dusk I went driving. On my way through the city I passed the Public Service building where Greta had worked. The sight of it did something to me. I turned into the entrance of the multi-storey car park just down the Terrace, stopped there for a while, and backed out. I couldn't make myself go in. From there I went across the bridge and found Blakey's house in the suburb by the river where all the doctors and the lawyers live and everything stinks of new money. Blakey's place was an open-front, glassy shoebox arrangement with the lights of the city on the river melting up towards it. Outside, I sat for some time. I don't know why I got out of the car. I was just doing things; my brain seemed a step behind every action.

I walked up the long, wide, curving driveway, found the double doors in a portico dense with bougainvillea, and rang the bell. A small woman came to the door. She looked drunk.

'Is Mr Blakey home?'

'No.' She leaned carefully on the door.

'When will he be back?'

'Are you a friend?'

'We have someone in common, I suppose.'

'He won't be back. We're divorced.'

She shut the big jarrah doors in my face.

All the way home I thought about Blakey, tried to remember what he looked like. He was taller than me and about as broad. Thick hair the colour of dead grass. He had a strong-featured face that was going to fat and he sat like a man who was used to sitting. At the trial, and at a work party where Greta introduced him to me once, he looked to me as though he'd only be comfortable at a desk or behind the wheel of a car. He talked a lot and loud.

The day after I visited Blakey's wife I did something I promised Greta and myself I would never do; I rang my old school friend Tony Mitchell. I knew then that I was serious. I really would kill Fred Blakey.

Tony Mitchell was an education officer at Fremantle Gaol. He'd made a lousy teacher in the state school system. I hadn't seen him since he began at Fremantle. He owed me a favour. In those early bare months after the trial, I sometimes wondered whether my old friend Tony Mitchell ever saw the man who raped my wife. I wanted to know what it was like for Blakey in prison; I needed to know he was scared and unpopular, but Greta didn't. The rape is over, I told myself; the man is in gaol. The past is the past. I determined never to use Tony Mitchell to satisfy my curiosity.

Tony Mitchell took a while to remember who I was.

When he did recognize me on the phone he sounded vexed, as though he deserved an explanation.

'What do you say to a drink?' I asked.

'Well—'

'Lunchtime tomorrow?'

'Been a long time, Neil.' Tony Mitchell was the only person alive who called me by my first name. Even Greta and my mother in Sydney called me Madigan.

The bar was crowded in the pub where we met in Fremantle. From it you could see the prison buttress above the tin rooftops of houses. Tony Mitchell had a stool saved for me at the corner of the bar. He was thin and looked as though he didn't know what to expect. We shook hands, made the tentative connections again. I bought him a few beers. He seemed worried.

'I need a favour,' I said after twenty minutes. 'As an old friend.'

He went stony. 'And it would have to be illegal.' Tony Mitchell owed me some favours. He had married young. Foolishly, I'd made him and his wife a whole dining suite for nothing because they were short of money; it took me months to recover financially.

'I don't know,' I said. 'Unethical, maybe.'

Tony fooled with his glass. 'You in trouble?'

I shook my head. 'You don't know my wife, do you? She was raped—'

'Madigan! I can't—'

'So you know him?'

'Shit, Madigan.' He drank off his beer and looked ready to leave. 'Yes, now that I've blurted it out. I know Fred Blakey.'

The old curiosity got me. 'What's he like inside?'

'He's all right. Getting old quick. Doing a degree in literature and politics externally.'

'Popular?'

'The screws like him. The boys like him well enough. Rapists aren't pick of the crowd inside.'

'He gets parole soon, doesn't he?'

'Madigan, I can't talk to you about Blakey. Give me a break.'

'All I want is some information. For a favour. You remember favours.'

'What're you gonna do? You can't dish out your own justice. Blakey's been punished. It has to stop somewhere.'

And I was thinking: What about for Greta, when does it finish for her? And me, when does my bloody life go back to normal, when do I get back everything that once belonged to me, for Chrissake?

'I'm not dishing out any justice.'

'How is your wife?'

'Fine.' I shrugged. 'I just want some information. I sort of know the guy – he's not a stranger. I thought I might clear the air.'

I bought him another drink, kept him on his seat. He looked hard at me. He didn't believe me for a moment.

'I just want to know when he gets out and what his address'll be outside. Just so I can contact him.'

'I'm sure he's in the phone book.'

'Didn't you hear about the divorce?'

'I'm in the business of helping guys improve themselves—'

'And I'm not gonna stand in the way of that.'

'I've got principles, Madigan.'

'Must be improving yourself, while you're at it. Things changed since the state schools, have they?'

He put down his beer. 'I've gotta be back.'

'One phone call.'

'Don't hold your breath,' he said, already walking.

I finished his beer and ordered myself another.

He rang three weeks later. Greta was beside me when I took the call; I felt her looking at me.

'June 12. Morning.' He hung up. That was all, but it was enough. I got to wondering why he did it at all. We were school mates and team mates from football. There was a favour outstanding. It was about a rape. We were men. I would have done the same.

Five weeks passed. Greta and I didn't speak much. We had the boys for a buffer. Greta had never been a weak person. She was independent – wilful even – when I married her. People said she wasn't afraid of men, of anybody. They liked her forthrightness and her kindness. I loved her for the way she looked and the way she could tell you to go to hell. She took charge of a situation. I just liked wood, happy to work as my own boss, confident that Greta and me had our own domains and the shared privacy of the house and the place our bodies made when we made love. We chatted and gossiped. We did things. People liked the sight of us together.

But those five weeks before Fred Blakey got out, we lay straight as nails in bed and Greta dressed in the dark and scratched herself and whimpered in her sleep. Doors were always locked and windows closed. Greta was no longer strong. I worked distractedly, got so far behind schedule that it seemed hopeless. All day I thought about Fred Blakey and at dinner Greta looked at me as though I might pounce at any moment.

46

The days were short and never warm. At night Greta sat with the twins in front of the TV until they were asleep, then she went to bed herself and I sat up alone, picking splinters from my palms. My body began to feel as though something had been hacked out of it.

One night I went in to bed and in the dark I heard her talking. I stopped before she heard me and I discovered that she was praying. I got into bed and hugged her hard. She yelped.

'Fred Blakey will pay, Greta,' I murmured in her ear. 'I swear it.'

She writhed free and I let her lie nail-straight beneath the quilt.

On the evening of June 11 I did two things. First I rang Tony Mitchell and he told me to go to hell. Someone, a woman, was shouting in the background. I'd had some Scotches; it was a bad idea to ring him. I had nothing to say to him in any case.

The second thing I did was more hopeful, but it went bad all the same. I took Greta out to an Italian place we'd been regulars at soon after we married. I drove her, organized the babysitter, opened doors for her. She needed to know I cared and understood.

We sat by the window with its ferns and baskets and bottles, watching people walk past to the cinemas and cafés. Across the way, a club washed the street the colour of sunset. I bought wine. The food was good: things in butter and rich sauces, pasta without meat on the sort of china we used to slip into handbags when things were tougher. Greta wore a light suit, all crushed and sultry-looking. The collar of bone beneath her throat was sweet to see. Her dark hair was short and showed her ears and that neck and I felt grateful for her. When she moved, in those nervous jerks she'd acquired, her breasts shifted and her hands furled and unfurled and it didn't seem so bad that there was no talk between us.

As we finished our coffee, Greta picked at breadcrumbs on the tablecloth and spoke quietly without looking up.

'What did you mean about Fred Blakey?'

Now that I looked at the top of her shirt I could see where she'd tried to disguise the ugly rash with powder.

'What I said. Only that he'd pay.' I smiled. 'I didn't know you had any religion.'

She continued to gather crumbs, eyes down. 'You wouldn't do anything stupid, would you?'

'I've done stupid things before.'

'If you ever—'

'You were praying. I heard you. What do you pray about?'

'I want to go home, Madigan.'

When we were out on the street, a dog ran from an alley and Greta shrieked, flattened herself against me, then after a moment, as the dog, running circles around the traffic lights, began to stop traffic, she unpicked herself from me and we walked back to the car like acquaintances.

June 12 was a Monday. By seven fifteen that morning, I was parked outside the football ground that backs on to Fremantle Gaol. Rain fell in short turns. There was no wind though I could smell the harbour plain enough. All the limestone buildings downtown looked pretty in the dull light with the sky behind. The long, high walls of the prison were of limestone also, but they were grim and no light, no weather could ever pretty them up.

No one seemed to take special notice of me. There was a hospital and some houses and the football ground close by, and the prison entrance was sixty metres down the hill, so my being there didn't need to seem suspicious.

I'd thought about what Blakey might do. If he was anything like me, he'd head straight down the hill for the nearest pub, walk those narrow streets to smell the fruit and coffee and see the women and the docks. Beside me on the seat of the rented car were a big wide roll of masking tape for the number plates, a stocking for my head and claw hammer in case of something unforeseen. When Fred Blakey came out on to the street and headed downtown, I would have plenty of time to tape up and disguise myself before running him down.

Cars came and went just after eight; the shift changing.

I wasn't nervous; I was like a lump of wood.

At nine twenty Fred Blakey drove past in a white VW with a woman at the wheel. The car came out of the entrance-way, turned up towards me and went past, going up the hill. They didn't appear to have seen me. I didn't know it was him until he was past and up round the bend. For a few moments I sat still, hands on the wheel. Then I started the little sedan and threw it into a U-turn up the hill.

A woman! I'd expected a broken man, spurned by all, shuffling out on the road, walking into Fremantle to survey his chances, here he was, the bastard, with a woman collecting him at the gate. I drove hard. I had no plan.

Around the bend the VW wasn't to be seen. The lumpy

road intersected with the north–south highway and on instinct I turned left to go north towards Perth. Buses and trucks stagnated the traffic. I found gaps, worked my way through, made good ground, and after a few minutes, I saw Blakey's car on a hill ahead. Eventually, I got within five cars of him and I kept my distance.

We wove round the river past shipyards and boatpens and yacht clubs until the better suburbs ran to the foreshore. I saw the two heads in the VW tilting towards one another in conversation, and all the time I tried to organize the business in my mind, to make some plan.

In time we reached the suburb where Blakey and his wife lived, but instead of passing through, as I expected, Blakey's girlfriend turned into a sidestreet away from the river and up through the trees and rich verges into a quiet avenue. I hung back without the cover of other cars. The VW slipped into a gravel drive between pines and I coasted past, got the number and drove home.

All day I sat alone in the workshop. Greta hung out the washing with the boys at her knee. When she reached up and exposed the back of her legs I saw her with Fred Blakey and I could hardly breathe. She saw the hire car later in the day, just looked hard at me and I kept away.

At dinner I joked with the twins and drank some beer. Greta brought out a lifeless vegetable casserole. She was remote. When she passed I had the feeling you get as a schoolboy when the prettiest girl in the class slides past: helplessness and gloom.

'Where did you go this morning?'

I said nothing. I wanted so much to talk. Later I said, 'Things'll get better. They will.'

For a moment her eyes lifted. The lines beneath them

made her older than she was. She looked tired and sick.
I wanted her. She turned to the twins, gave them toneless
baby talk and supervised their meal.

Late the same evening I parked in the street where I'd
left Fred Blakey earlier in the day. In the dark, I walked
past a few times until I had an idea of the place. It was a
closed-in kind of house, thick with trees and shrubs, every
kind of creeper, rockeries, retaining walls, small pools of
lawn. Not a vast place, but very comfortable; it made mine
look quaint.

I took the stocking and hammer with me when I finally
went down between those pines towards the house. The
grass was wet and quiet. Neighbouring houses were
obscured by walls and vegetation, so I had no reasonable
fear of being observed.

The first window I came to had a faint light in it. It
seemed to be a living room: couches, a roaring stereo,
standard lamp, and a sleeping dog. The stereo saved me; the
dog seemed overwhelmed by Elton John. I couldn't match
up Fred Blakey with Elton John. Mantovani, perhaps.

I picked through the garden to other windows, but they
were dark and had the curtains drawn. From out there the
manic piano of the record sounded weird and set my nerves
awry. The final window, a big-paned bay window, was
carelessly draped with a faint pink light sifting out. I eased
up from a crouch in the flowerbed and saw through gaps in
the curtains that the room was a bedroom and occupied.

I saw two pairs of legs. The man's were hairy, varicose
and white. The woman's were shorter, darker, younger. I
tried another space in the drapes and saw a profile of the

woman's face against the hairy white shoulder of a man. She didn't look twenty years old. Her hair was blonde and cut short. She had full lips and a small jaw. Her eyes were closed. I couldn't hear what she said when her lips moved. At another space in the curtains I saw the man's heaving back. I saw him stiffen, roll aside. The man was Fred Blakey. He looked old, with the roadmap face of a drinker, and with his greying hair all scuffed up, he looked forlorn.

I stood in the garden with the claw hammer in my hand and one of Greta's stockings wrapped round my wrist. I saw that heaving white back on Greta, saw his smooth old hands pushing her head into the concrete, the spittle at the corners of his mouth, her breasts strangling in his fists, those places I knew he'd dribbled over, the stain of his big white body on me.

Greta would be in bed by now. Her body would be shut tight; she'd be lying there hard and straight in our bed where things used to be whole and sweet. Maybe she'd be scratching her rash, or praying like a scared kid, cold and straight. And in there, twelve hours out of gaol, was Fred Blakey heaving and lurching on a girl who seemed to enjoy it. He had hair on his shoulders. I turned the hammer over in my hands. I went out to my hired car and waited.

About midnight the lights went out in the house where Fred Blakey was. At one thirty the streetlights went out. The radio in the car put me to sleep. I dreamt I was walking down a passage that got narrower and narrower. I ran down it, faster, crazier. When I woke it was four thirty. I switched off the radio. The windows were opaque with condensation

52

and the ceiling of the car was wet. I opened a window, cold air rushed in, my head cleared.

Suddenly I felt sad, as though something had slipped from my grasp. I sat like that, like a bereaved man, until six fifty when Fred Blakey and the girl jogged out on to the road with the small dog. They wore red tracksuits.

I hadn't planned this. I hadn't planned anything. My mind was bogged. I just acted.

When they were out of sight down the hill, I tried to start the car, but it wouldn't catch. I kept trying. I was calm; I didn't curse. I let off the handbrake, took the car out of gear and rolled. At the fourth hop, the motor started. I revved it hard and braked. I waited a full minute. I couldn't have told you my name.

By the time I caught them up, Fred Blakey and the girl and the dog were at the road by the river. It was the side away from the river. He was on the grass verge. She was on the road. The dog zigzagged between them. She turned and fell, mouth wide, as I rode up the kerb behind them, but Blakey never turned around. She went under. Something flew off to the side.

Blakey rose out of the ground and starwheeled up over the bonnet and I felt him thwacking across the roof and down the boot, and then I was around the bend, collecting sprinklers and the edges of parked cars, trying to get back on the road. There was mist on the river and skyscrapers looked like giants rearing from clouds.

I went in quiet at home. Greta woke as I crawled in beside her. She rose on an elbow and looked at me through sleep-narrow eyes. The look on her face. She hid her breasts. She got out of bed, pulling on a shaving coat and jerked up the blind. A small sound hicked in her throat. The morning light flattened me.

'It's all right, now,' I murmured.

'No, Madigan,' she said. 'It's not.'

And in that moment I knew that I had lost my life. I was a dead man.

Distant Lands

The girl they called Fat Maz worked in her father's news-agency. Her father had a club foot and he was an angry man because the army had never wanted him. All day he clomped up and down between the racks of magazines keeping an eye out for thieves and making sure people bought things instead of standing and reading for free. The girl's mother sat all day at the register and watched the cars pass. Once a day a big Greyhound rolled past going north to the city. Only the dull drumming of the old National reminded the girl that her mother was there. She was always relieved when her parents went home for lunch and left the shop to her.

Every day at the lunch hour, a tall dark man came in, paused for a moment just inside the door as if to adjust his eyes or to get his bearings before heading straight to the paperback novel called *Distant Lands*, opened it, and with his foot on the bottom shelf, read for fifteen minutes. The first time he came in his reading was furtive; he spent as much time looking up to see if he was being watched as he did reading. His eyes showed white and worried over the burst of exotic purple on the cover, and to show that she couldn't have cared less, the girl smiled at him and shrugged.

'Interesting?' she asked that first day as he walked out without spending a cent.

The man said nothing. He just passed the register with his eyes downcast. When he got out in the street, he adjusted his tie, buttoned his jacket against the smelly harbour breeze, and went.

After that, the man came again, but he did not look at the girl or give any sign of recognition. Her father would have thrown him out. Not only was he freeloading; she guessed he was a Pakistani too. His Nescafé hands were clean and well manicured. His suit was conservative and cut sharp. When she inspected *Distant Lands* she saw that he had marked his place with a long, black hair. The book looked as though it had never been opened. On the back cover, the blurb said: *You will want this book never to finish.*

As weeks passed, the girl wondered whether she should read *Distant Lands* for herself. The dark man seemed to draw such energy from it; she could see it in the way he buttoned his jacket against the wind each day. But the book was so long and she'd hardly read a book since leaving school, and, besides, she felt somehow as though it might be eavesdropping. For now, it was enough just to look forward to the lunch hour and that strange feeling of comradeship she felt when the dark man was in the shop. She was part of a conspiracy. For an hour, her rules were shop rules. Just watching him up the back with his polished shoe on the lower shelf and the gloss finish of his down-pointed brow shining in the fluorescent light gave her pleasure.

She was not a sporty girl. She did not read. She had no boyfriend. Sometimes she would bicycle out to the edge of town and look along the highway. She felt herself growing fatter every day. She hated the smell of the harbour and she often wondered whether she smelt of it after all these years.

Several times she almost asked the man how the book was coming along, and once she nearly left the register to confront him, ask him why he read it at all, but even as she opened her mouth or got up from her seat, she knew she might spoil lunch hours for them both. For even though he never even met her gaze after the first day, and even though they'd never really conversed and he'd never actually bought a single item from the newsagency, the girl knew they understood one another. She had never felt this tacit understanding with anyone before.

Once the dark man came in late. The girl's parents had come back from lunch. She felt her arse tighten. She saw the dark man walk down to the back, oblivious. She held her breath. But before he even touched *Distant Lands* the man seemed to sense the girl's mother craning over the National, and he left immediately. He was back next day, dead on time.

There was a more serious crisis. One day, a big red woman in a shiny cardigan brought *Distant Lands* to the register. At the time, the girl's mother was out on the pavement dragging in wet bundles of the *Daily News*.

'I'm sorry,' the girl said. 'That book's reserved.'

'What's this – a libr'y?' The big red woman deepened a tone.

'It's on order. Sorry.' It seemed desperately important to save it for tomorrow's lunch hour. It might take weeks to get another copy down from the city and the thought of lunch hour without a visit from the stranger sent a gallop of panic through her.

'Haven't you got more?' The big woman put a meaty beringed hand upon the register.

'I'm really sorry.'

The woman stood there for a moment as though deciding tactics, but in the end she slapped the book down on the glass counter and rolled out. At the sight of the great rump in retreat, the girl felt fear. That could be me, she thought. It wasn't the fatness so much as the . . . the . . . whatever it was that seemed so patently missing. The woman hadn't even really wanted the book, she began to suspect. Their little confrontation was just something to do.

She watched her mother drag in the newspapers. Her father passed, throwing his foot angrily ahead of him. Outside the Greyhound was pulling away empty.

As she helped close up that night, she felt the oddest seesawing inside her. By dinner it was gone and she watched TV until she slept where she sat.

Next morning she felt guilty. She had no friends, but her mother and father looked after her. They'd given her a job when she quit school, and jobs were impossible to get in this little town. Maybe things weren't as bad as all that.

That day, the dark man came in as usual. Watching him read, she noted that he was not handsome, though she did not object to his colour. His teeth had the look of polished rice. She felt a smile wedge her face as he turned a page. Was that little snapping movement in him excitement? Now she was happy; there was no doubt of it. This was happiness, not everything else.

The shop was empty. There was only the dark man reading *Distant Lands* and her peering openly at him over the register. Nothing else but a thousand garish glossy covers. He's happy, she thought, seeing him turn another page.

As she watched, the Nescafé coloured man turned what

she'd swear looked like the last page. Her throat closed her heart off. She heard him sigh. She saw him shut the book and place it back on the shelf. She saw him coming to the register.

His small teeth showed in a smile.

'Thank you,' he said.

The girl opened her mouth.

'And this is for the bus,' he said, putting a note on her palm. 'Goodbye.'

The girl they called Fat Maz watched him go out into the main street, turn his collar against the harbour wind, and go on his way.

After a moment, she went down to the back of the shop. She was excited and confused. *Distant Lands* stood on the shelf. She picked up a long black hair. It was strong enough to wind around her finger like a tourniquet and turn the flesh blue. She stood with her back to the shelf and let out a grunt. The fifty-dollar note was starchy-new. She stuffed it down her jumper and into her bra. Leaning against the shelf for a moment, she looked towards the door. When she breathed, the money sounded electric between her breasts.

She met her parents at the door. She saw shadows in their brows. She fairly crackled.

Laps

1

After seven years, Queenie Cookson began to swim
seriously again. Each morning she drove to City Beach and
swam up and down between the groynes. Out behind
garlands of surfers and waist-deep swimmers, she scored the
swells with her strokes. It hurt; she felt as though she was
etching herself on the sea. As she tilted her head to breathe,
she would often see on the beach her husband and daughter
keeping pace. All this time, she thought, they've been
growing, and I've gone to fat. It took her seven years to find
will again, to shrug off defeat.

She had come from her home town a loser, an outcast;
she left behind a grave and a crusade and a well of bitterness,
and somehow she'd turned her mind to being a mother and
relearning how to be married. These things were good
shelters. But seven years of softness hadn't taken all will
from her. Queenie Cookson did not like to be beaten. She
did not like to cower. Her big, brown body and everything
that lived in it was not trained to be that way. In the first
month of summer she lost ten kilograms, and she knew she
could be hard again.

Every stroke of her dogged freestyle was a blow, and with each swim she knew she was shifting more than her own weight. Somehow, out there that summer, Queenie changed. Early on, the morning swim was like doing penance, but in time it became a pleasure. She began to feel she belonged in the dawn-brown sea, as she had when she was a girl, when her grandfather was alive, when the world could only be good. The old man had taught Queenie to swim. He threw her out of the dinghy and rowed just ahead, calling, coaxing, hounding her. He was all she had. She'd left him buried on a hill she no longer owned.

These mornings, Cleve and Dot mooned along the beach indulging her. Sometimes Dot paddled out on her board and Cleve watched her hassling for waves with men twice her size. It made him laugh to see her cut a long bottom turn; she was dwarfed by the most puny wave. She put the men to shame zigging and zagging under the churning weight of water. Cleve stopped joggers and pointed her out. He could not let her go unnoticed.

Like her mother, Dot swam before she could talk. Her short honey hair was cut and shaped like a mushroom and her skin was the colour of sherry. She had the body of a miniature athlete. She was six years old. Though a strong swimmer, she was lazy like Cleve, and swimming laps bored her motionless. Most mornings, unless the swell was good, she just walked with Cleve, not saying much. Both of them would prefer to be at Scarborough; it was just down the hill from where they lived and the surf was better, but it was safer at City Beach for laps, and besides, the little men with big money were tearing up the beachfront to build hotels for the Americans and neither of them could stand the sight of the cranes and steel skeletons and hard-hats and the awful wound in the ground where the burger joints and pinball parlours had been.

'They're tearing up the fount of my youth,' Cleve would say and wave his arms like a Shakespearean actor.

Dot would shove her hands into her pockets and drop her head. 'They're making a rotten mess.'

So out of duty, and with sadness, they went with Queenie to City Beach.

One morning, near the end of summer, as Cleve handed her a towel, Queenie shook the water from herself and told him she was ready now.

'For what? What are you ready for, more laps?' He elbowed Dot.

'Ready to go back.'

'Where?' Dot screwed up her face and sucked on the strap of her bathers. 'Cor, swimming.'

'Back to Angelus, Cleve.' The soberness of her tone surprised even her. Weighty. Yes, she thought, there's weight to lose.

'A holiday?' Dot straightened.

Queenie smiled. 'A weekend, maybe. You might see a whale. They're coming back there, these days. It was where we used to live. It's my home town. We had a different life, then, Dot.' She noticed Cleve's old apprehensive habit of kicking the sand. 'I've been thinking about it all summer, Cleve, and I reckon it's time. We can't avoid it any more. We're older. Places shouldn't frighten us any more. We got screwed by the place – OK. But a place can't screw you for ever. It'd help me, Cleve.'

She saw his face set. Dot looked from her to him. They all walked up the blenching beach to the car park. The sky and the easterly gave warning of another withering day.

Summer: watermelon, flyscreen doors, sleeping on the back lawn in the haze of mosquito coils, the sweet smell of water on dying grass, undisciplined sunsets. It was what they lived for.

No one spoke on the way home in the rattling Land Rover. The Cooksons lived in a little weatherboard house, thick with passionfruit and grape vines, on the hill above Scarborough Beach. It *was* a new life they had here. The hurt of seven years before had healed them together in a way they had not expected. It was only lately Queenie had come to notice it. She had been numb for longer than she could recall.

Dot stomped from room to room, getting ready for school. Cleve fried eggs on the gas range. Queenie fingered the ever-dull *West Australian* on the table. She didn't pretend to be happy.

'You don't agree then,' she said.

Her hands before her were big and salt-wrinkled. The kitchen smelled of potted herbs and last night's fish batter. She looked at Cleve's peeling shoulders. He was thinking hard, she knew. His legs were too thin for him; it looked as though the bottom half of him went hungry. He didn't seem afraid of turning thirty-two next week.

Dot crashed in and sat down.

'Sunny side, Dad.'

'Why?'

Queenie prepared herself. Breakfast. Banter.

The little girl replied: 'Cause I like the yellow dot.'

'A flaming *dot*. That's what we got.'

'A dot. So what?'

'Yeah, could have been worse. Imagine twins. Twin dots. A colon. Three, an ellipsis.'

Dot pouted.

'Not those lips, dill. If you were twenty dots I could get a pair of scissors and cut along the line.'

She made a sound of a fart with her mouth.

'But all we got was one lousy Dot. A dot with a bot.'

'The whole world is a dot. From a long way.'

'So is an egg. Here, eat it. Actually, an egg is a world, too, for a while.' But Cleve had lost her. Dot had punctured the yolk and was tamping it with wads of buttered toast.

Queenie watched him back at the stove. He knew she was watching, but it didn't spoil the morning's ritual. Queenie saw him shuffle around the kitchen. He had changed a lot. She liked him so much more since Dot was born and they'd lived here. He was frumpish and good, these days; he'd stopped trying to be someone he never was, now he had no country mettle to prove. She imagined people would like him at the hospital where he lifted them and wheeled them through the labyrinth into the operating room or out the big glass doors to freedom.

She received her egg and a kiss on the brow.

'You don't agree, then?'

Cleve sat down and bit into a big, green capsicum. 'Yeah, let's go tomorrow.'

'For the weekend?' Dot wore a dag of yolk on her chin.

Cleve nodded. Queenie laughed and was afraid.

2

As soon as Dot was home from school, the Cooksons left for Angelus.

Just after sunset, near the town of Williams, they hit a

kangaroo and Cleve had to get out and kill it with the wheelbrace. It took five hours' driving to get to the small town on the south coast. When the lights of the town rose from the dark like a new galaxy, Cleve woke Dot and she watched dumbly.

Angelus was no longer a whaling town. These days it lived by farm produce and traded hard on its English climate. Tourists came to see its awesome cliffs and beaches, the wildflowers in their season, the museums, the relics. Angelus had learnt to live off its dying. No one mentioned the protest any more. It was a town looking bright-faced into the future.

The motel Queenie checked them into had a spouting concrete whale in its floodlit forecourt. Their room stale, drab. It stank of cigarette smoke and Pine-O-Clean. Dot fiddled with the TV and the motel notepaper, flicked through the Gideon Bible without enthusiasm and went to sleep. Cleve and Queenie turned the light out for her and sat in the dark. Cleve pulled some cans from the smelly little refrigerator and they drank beer in silence.

Pubs closed. They listened to the sound of men weaving up the street to their wives.

'Nothing's changed,' Queenie whispered.

'We have.'

'Are we any better, do you think?'

'We try harder,' said Cleve.

'I suppose we should see everything.'

'I guess it's the point of the exercise. Exorcize.'

'I just want to come back and see the place and be normal in it. And maybe see Poppa's grave. I want to . . . confirm things.'

'Like what?'

'Like us growing up. Like us being properly together. Like this town being the past.'

Fresh from their antiseptic motel breakfast, the Cooksons went out into the bright, windy morning, and without much sense of purpose or direction, began to walk. Fat clouds bundled up from the south. The air was mild; it was not the summer they had left. As they turned into the main street, the steel surface of the harbour came into view.

'Pretty,' Dot said.

Queenie put a hand on Dot's mushroom head.

'Yep. Pretty.' It was. It still was. Queenie saw it better than she ever had.

All morning they visited familiar places: park benches, a certain rose garden, some historic cottages, delicatessens. All morning Queenie hardened herself. Sooner or later someone would recognize her, she knew. She just had to tough it out. But no one did. And as the morning proceeded, anonymity began to peeve her. No one recognized her as Queenie Coupar the local girl who turned coat; she was just another tourist come to see the wildflowers and replicas and plaster whales.

Cleve took them out to the deep-water jetty to show Dot the tiny shack where he huddled when he was a watchman, when his life was creaking and falling around him. It was a long walk to the end. Some boys fished. Down on a landing near the water, two old drunks lay in each other's arms and the morning sun set alight the dew on their backs.

'Was it cold?' Dot asked.

'Yes.' Queen answered for him. She recalled the fights, the hardness between them, the emptiness of the bed at night.

'Rats used to crawl everywhere,' said Cleve.

'Ugh.'

'A man jumped off here and drowned one night,' Queen said.

'Yes. One night.'

Dot went to the edge with a wrinkle on her brow.

'It's hard to understand I know,' Queenie said.

Dot nodded. Gulls stitched the sky behind. Queenie felt as though all this was a story she had read somewhere; it didn't seem part of her life.

By midday the harbour lost its sheen. The Cooksons ate lunch in a quiet pub with a view of the water. Queenie felt Cleve watching her as they all chattered and rattled cutlery. Below them was the town jetty where the tugs and official craft berthed. Once it had been the mooring for the whale chasers.

'This is a nice town,' Dot said. She stuffed a chip into her little oval mouth. 'I'd like to live here.'

Queenie felt herself flinch. 'Wait till you see the beaches. The beaches are the whitest, the cleanest . . .'

'Cleaner 'n' brider an' bigger 'n' wider,' Cleve said in an American drawl.

Dot giggled. Two men in business suits left off dismantling their T-bones and looked at Cleve with open suspicion.

'Oops,' Cleve whispered. 'The accent. They think we're greenies. Let's not talk French either, eh? Let's just be rubbernecks for the day.'

'It's all we ever were, Cleve.' Queenie pulled back her bread-coloured hair.

'No,' he said. 'We cared about things. No one can take that away.'

On the crest of a hill, Cleve pulled up before the tall timber house. It seemed to have been dug into the granite flank of the hill. It was old and solid and lovely. An English house. At the sight of it, Queenie felt the veins in her neck thicken.

'This is where we used to live,' she murmured to Dot who was sleepy and listless.

'Why didn't I ever live there?'

'You weren't born then,' Cleve said. 'It used to belong to Queenie's family. Like the farm.'

'Now it doesn't.'

'Oh!'

'Yeah. Oh.' Cleve looked at her. She smiled.

'Houses don't matter, though, do they, Dot?'

'Ya just live in um, that's all.'

'Glad you came, Spot,' Cleve said. 'You're good counsel.'

'I'm tired.'

Queenie pulled her springy little body across the seat and put her head in her lap.

'I learnt to swim in this town, Dot. When I did everything else lousy. I knew I could always get in the water and swim like a fish. Like you.'

'I surf, Mum.'

'Yeah. Well.'

Queenie looked away from the old house. Someone had opened a curtain. Cleve put the Land Rover into gear.

Despite the sombre afternoon light, the beaches along the peninsula glowed. They struck Queenie as almost gaudy in their whiteness.

Dot slept, but Queenie still addressed remarks to her, even though they were meant for Cleve.

'Yep. Learnt to make love here, too, Dot. And I learnt to stick to my guns no matter what. An' then I learnt about how stupid it can be to stick to your guns after your ammo's run out.'

68

Cleve smiled. 'I wanted to be a hero too, you know.'

'Now you're just a dag. Thank God.'

'Cheer up. This is the good bit coming up.'

'You know we didn't stop the killing.'

'You helped stop it. That's enough. Jesus, you're so proud.'

Queenie smiled. 'Yeah. One thing I did inherit.'

Dot awoke at Paris Bay where the huge, rusting oil tanks still stood. As they coasted down the long hill overlooking the Sound, Queenie saw the tiny whalers' cabins, the fallen jetty, some paint-smeared sheds, and she was full of memories.

A caretaker met them at the gate and took two dollars from them. 'We're making the place into a museum, since the bastards closed us down,' he said. 'Been here before?'

'A long time ago,' said Cleve. He found himself grinning and he caught Queenie's eye.

And there it was. The long ramp of the flensing deck where once Queenie had lain in the blood and offal with the others, the cogs, the great windlasses, the chimneys from the boilers, the oily shorebreak. Beside the ruined jetty, the *Paris II* was aground and bloody with rust, the harpoon gun up-tilted on the bow.

As they walked on to the flensing deck, Cleve was grim-faced. Queenie was surprised to discover in herself a sadness for the place. She had campaigned so bitterly to destroy it. Now there were only gulls and wind. It was pathetic.

'Hey, check this out!' Cleve called to them from the base of a vast tank. It stood forty feet high and silver paint came off in great shaley leaves. Cleve turned a wheel and a circular hatch squawked open.

When they reached him, only his legs showed from the little hatch. His voice thundered inside the tank.

'Let me in, Dad.'

'No, Dotty, it's a bit smelly,' Queenie said.

'Used to be full of whale oil.'

'Bet it took a million litres. Let me in, Dad.'

The legs disappeared and after a moment Cleve's face poked out. 'Here.'

'Cleve.'

'It's all right. Come on, mate.' He pulled the child in and she let out a gasp.

'Cor.' Her footsteps echoed. The tank vibrated. 'Come in, Mum. It's mint.'

Queenie stood outside with her back to the flaking metal. Some weak sun came out and retreated. She heard Cleve and Dot charging about inside. Every now and then she caught a hint of the unforgettable stench of burning blubber. But the place was dead; she knew it now.

'All right,' she shouted into the hatch. 'Enough.'

As they walked back up the gravel drive, Dot grabbed her hand and Cleve's and the wind blew and she was like a sail between them.

Then there was only the farm to see. They didn't stop now; Queenie knew if they stopped they'd never drive out there and she'd never be satisfied. It rained. On the old road parrots sputtered green and the sky hung low and they hissed through sheets of fallen water. Rich milking pasture gave way to a more austere landscape where sheep stood still. Oh, she knew that land, that road.

On the farm gate hung a sign. NO TRESPASSERS. ROO SHOOTERS SHOT. KEEP OUT. In a century and a half no one had put a sign up before. No one had been denied entry to this place. Cleve and Queenie sat dumb in the idling vehicle. Beyond the gate, the rising land was overgrazed and guttered. In the distance, the hill showed signs of tree-felling.

'A hundred and fifty years,' Queenie murmured. 'And now this.'

'We'll talk to them, tell them who you are.'

They opened the gate and drove up the bone-shaking track to the old house where they were met by a thin, red man with amber freckles. Queenie felt it all: the smell of wet soil, hay, the slummocky sounds of cattle, the stone house built by her ancestors, the windmill where she'd climbed as a girl . . . she was dizzy with it. The man waited for neither respect nor explanation.

'You saw the sign. Get the hell off.'

'My wife's Queenie Coupar.'

'I know who she is. Get off.'

'She just wants to see the old man's grave. It's on the hill.'

'Mr Pustling's orders are for no one to—'

'He doesn't own the grave, for Chrissake!' Queenie began.

'Then you'll need a helicopter to land on that six foot of ground, lady. Get off the place.'

'C'mon, Cleve.'

'We should have known better,' Cleve said when they were outside the gate again. Queenie got out to close it.

'I want to go home,' Dot said.

'Let me drive, Cleve.'

He looked at her a moment and got out. She got in behind the wheel.

'What about the gate?'

'Leave it open.'

71

Dot and Cleve exchanged looks. The farmhouse was obscured by trees and rising ground. There was no one near. Queenie swung the Land Rover around and back through the gate into the firebreak along the inside of the fence.

'We're going to the beach, anyway. Stuff 'em.'

'She used to be like this all the time, Dot.'

'She drives like a loony.'

The beach spread itself white between two granite headlands. Queenie churned the Land Rover past places where she had played and loitered. She met Cleve on this beach; he'd been a trespasser once before. Dot was conceived here. And a few years later, this was where everything came aground. A pod of whales. The Coupar line. Their marriage.

'This is a special place, Dot,' she said, pulling up near the tidal smear of weed.

'No,' said Cleve, 'it's just a beach. Just a place.'

She looked at him a moment. 'Yes. You're right.'

It started to rain again. Queenie pulled off her T-shirt. She had the back and shoulders of a rower. Wholemeal hair settled back on her shoulders.

'I think she's gonna swim,' Cleve said, and dug Dot in the ribs.

Dot rolled her eyes. 'More laps.'

Queenie jogged down to the water, breasts beating, and dived into the shorebreak. She bellied into the path of a breaker, pierced its back and struck out to calmer water where she floated and waved. Up behind the vehicle on the deserted beach she saw the dunes. Further back was the hulking shadow of the hill where the old man was buried. In his own six feet. Well, that's all anyone needs, she thought. More than I need.

She launched into a crawl, smacking across the tops of

swells as she had done behind the old man in the boat all those years back. She kept the hill in sight. She struck out, not invincible but strong. And she knew she could swim it all out of her; it was only a matter of time.

Bay of Angels

I sat with him by the river. The big, sad peppermints gave us shade and the breezy scent of their litter. Across the rumpled water, on the opposite bank, freeway traffic glittered in miniature and city towers took the white sun on their flanks. Full-bellied yachts were passing; they floated by like light and music. There were children near us, and gulls. It was beautiful to see. But I knew my friend saw nothing. There are times when all you can do is feel, when there's nothing but alarms ringing and you can't even see yourself in the mirror.

I sat by, in the world outside him.

'Ah, God, the water,' I said. 'My grandmother called this the Bay of Angels.'

My friend gave an all but imperceptible nod.

'I can't think why,' I said.

I sat with him. Neither of us was young any more. I couldn't see those nerves blue-sparking in him, but I knew it was happening. I took off my shirt and saw again that I was tanned and going to fat. What the hell, I thought guiltily; who cares.

I sat outside of my friend and waited for him to tell it all to me. That's why we were there. He said these afternoons helped him stay float; it was like jettisoning cargo. His mother looked after his wife and kids once a week, and in return she expected him to cope.

I learnt to walk on that soft strip of sand by the water. My mother took me down there as a baby. In all the photos we're brown as nuts and she looks like that old film star, Esther Williams.

I thought: It's safe here – next week I'll bring little Sam down.

I was waiting to hear it all.

My friend was trying to understand, but he just didn't know what it meant to seize up altogether. Though I heard him speak of it, he'd never been unable to continue the way a swimmer, cramped up and beaten, prepares to drown. Thinking about it made my mouth taste electric. I remembered that year, hiding out in the bush. I remembered the four walls of that hut and the suggestions of the sea and the lapping of family voices and the ultramarine light slowly deepening inside.

But today I was alive enough to be going to fat and to see the city as beautiful. I felt grateful and, somehow, guilty for not being able to explain myself.

'Want a dip?' I asked.

My friend took off his singlet. He was white and not going to fat. What the hell.

We waded out. The cool water was stained from its path through the hills but it was clean. We breast-stroked out towards the line of moored boats. I dived to the bottom and came up laughing.

'Middle of a city and it's clean water!'

My friend cut the water beside me.

From there it seems as though the city block was resting

on water. Kings Park sat green above it. The sky was the colour of sleep. I rolled on my back and saw the old university, pretty and fatuous in its nest of foliage. At night the shores here would germinate with the light of lamps and the sound of people laughing and wading with nets and calling after children. There would be fires and the smell of cooking prawns, the hiss of beer-cans, faint music and the commotion of somebody stung by a cobbler. There would be cars revving. There would be the dark way of the water.

And I forgot I was swimming, supporting myself in water. My friend laboured beside me. Sobered, I said, 'We always come back to water. When things happen.'

I waited for my friend to tell me, but he stroked along eyes shuttered against the sun.

Swimming back through the boats, we came upon a yacht swathed in nets to keep children off. Hanging strangled in the net, a gull swung above the water like a cheap symbol in a film. I swam wide. I sensed my friend tiring; his stroke was ragged.

We scattered tiny smelt before us in the shallows as we waded in.

We sat on towels.

'C'mon,' I said. 'Is she worse?' He had kids. He believed in a God somewhere. His wife always told mine he was good in bed.

We sat there a long time, and as I waited for it all to come out I saw a host of white-sailed yachts sweeping down in the wind. Bay of Angels. The sails were like the wings of Angels. My heart fattened with joy.

My friend began to weep.

I sat there with my mouth open.

The strong one

1

One morning at the beginning of summer, Rachel left them asleep and walked down through the peppermints to the caretaker's office to post her letter. The office had wide plate windows pasted with maps and announcements. She stopped to witness her reflection in the glass. She looked good. Her skin was clear, there was light in her hair, and when she put her hand against her belly it looked as firm as it felt. The ponderous weight of her breasts was gone. She had survived something to become Rachel again. No; she knew she was more.

The caretaker took her letter and slipped it under the old hinge he used as a paper weight and a filing system. He looked at the city address.

'The university, eh?'

'Applying for social work.'

For a moment his eyes settled on the front of her T-shirt where her nipples stood out dumb from the morning chill. He was a short, dark man. In his fifties, she guessed, with a strangely turned foot. It seemed that every caravan park they stayed in was run by lame men. Rachel wondered how it must be for him to gimp across the grass every morning knowing that from behind curtains in caravans all around, people were watching, discussing.

'Well, good luck to yer.' He smiled up into her face and she felt no malice. 'Hubby studying?'

Rachel shook her head.

When she got back, she heard little squeals of glee. She climbed the step of the sagging, rented van. It was small. There was no way to keep it tidy.

Jerra looked up. He was still in bed. Sam straddled his chest, shrieking. An arc of drool fell on Jerra's chest like a little silver lasso.

'He's teething again,' Jerra said.

Rachel filled the kettle and lit the gas. 'I applied. Sent it just now.'

Jerra sucked Sam's fingers. 'Uh-huh.'

Rachel licked her lips. 'Could we live on a student's allowance, you reckon? What is it, these days, less than the dole?'

'Dunno.'

She watched him blow on the child's wet fingers to make him giggle. He did it purposefully, without humour.

'God knows,' he said, 'we barely survive on the dole.'

'Maybe your mum and dad'd help us out.'

Jerra pushed Sam's glistening hand away. He looked at her. 'You know what I think about that.'

Rachel shrugged. He didn't know that she'd had a cheque from his parents every month since the winter. She'd come to love the Nilsams. They were good people, not like her own parents at all. She couldn't understand Jerra's attitude towards them. She knew there'd been problems when he was younger, but it was so long ago. Jerra seemed to bear weights from the past as though they were treasures he had to take with him. It made no sense. She'd had to jettison more than he had to stay afloat: the lousy luggage of family memory, the self-hatred other men had seized upon and cultivated – even bearing Sam and having him torn out by force. She knew how good Jerra had been for her. He'd helped her to free herself, only she wondered if he'd ever want it for himself. And lately she'd come to suspect he enjoyed bearing it all, as though the past, as well as being his source of pain, might also be his only source of comfort. One day she'd drive it all out of him. One day.

'Maybe I could play a few wine bars.'

She snorted. 'Music.' Even she was surprised at the level of contempt in her voice. Their eyes met. 'No, I s'pose you're right.'

Sam squirmed. They both watched him. Rachel felt them drinking up the sight of him.

'Jerra?'

'Yeah?'

'I really want this. The studying, I mean. You know I never had a chance before. You always said I'd go back and do something one day. I'm ready now. I've had enough of this kind of living. It was good to come here. There was nowhere else to go. But I'm better now. And I'm tired of toilet seats warmed by other people's bums, and I'm tired of standing in other people's shower water when the drains're blocked. I had ten years of that when I was a kid. It's time to go, Jerra.'

'The mill. What if . . .?'

His voice trailed off as she sat down. There was no anger in her. She spoke out of a weird, sensible calm.

'I've followed you round a long time now, Jerra. The band, these other jobs. Now that Sam's weaned and I'm well again . . . well, I reckon it's time you followed me for a while.'

Jerra held Sam by the leg. She saw his thumb traverse firm, sweet skin. A lawn mower started up across the park.

Rachel tried to get eye contact again, but he was intent on Sam.

'I mean, at least you know what you're good at—'

'Even if it is a total bloody dead-end.'

'Well, at least you had a chance to find out. While you were cruising up and down the coast in a Kombi, I—'

'All right. You're right. Let's not expose my piddling middle-class self-pity.'

Suddenly, Sam seemed alarmed and reached for her. She smiled to reassure him. He put his hands slowly into his lap and looked at them in wonder. Rachel ran a hand across her belly again. She'd get out into the sun this summer and tan that skin till those marks were fine and silver as fishbones, yes, that's what she'd do.

'What'll I do?' Jerra asked. 'If you study.'

'Look after Sam.'

His eyes narrowed and she saw him let go of Sam. It was only a moment.

'Me? I can't.'

'You what!'

'I mean . . . I'm not—'

'A woman?' She got his eyes at last. He looked trapped.

'No, that's not what I—'

'Hell, Jerra.'

She saw him look away.

'Isn't it good enough for you, looking after a baby? All that talk!'

He turned back. There was heat in his face. Rachel stood and laughed. And then for a moment she thought he might actually begin to cry.

'Well, what then?'

'Can't you see? I'm scared, that's all. That I won't be able to do it properly.'

She pounced on him and drove her teeth into his shoulder. He yelped and Sam fell back on the bed.

'How do you think I felt? Eh?'

She lay across him and watched him lie there with his eyes darting. She felt she could burst with anger and tenderness at any moment. A neat moon of welts darkened on his skin.

2

As they walked out along the road to the beach on Christmas morning, Rachel wondered if it would ever happen, if there'd ever be a change for the better. The past two years seemed such a mess: the band folding, the pregnancy they couldn't decide to end, the lousy odd-jobs, and the illness and frailty of the last, long winter. Jerra was stiff and hard with surviving; sometimes she didn't know him at all. He seemed happy still to mark time, as though he wasn't ready yet for another battle. But Rachel was bursting, ready to act.

Sam burbled and spat. They took turns wheeling him. The road was flanked by the estuary on one side and the bush on the other. It wasn't hot enough for a swim, but even when it was cool these days they walked down to the rivermouth to sit and watch the sea move and sigh and disguise itself in the glitter of sunlight; it gave shape to the day. Waiting, Rachel thought as she pushed; all this bloody waiting. But it didn't feel so futile any more, now that there was something real to wait for.

The estuary was full. It was the colour of strong tea. Near the mouth, the limestone faces of the cliffs looked hollow and wracked by morning shadows. The scent of river mud stood in the air.

Jerra took off his shirt. He was getting his tan back. She'd seen photos of him nearly black from the sun. The roasted darkness of him made him appear bigger than he was, and, narrowed in the sun, his eyes bore the shuttered shape of obsession. But those were old photos from his teens. Mrs Nilsam had shown her. Rachel knew they'd worry her if she looked at them long enough.

'See that track?' He pointed to a faint break in the vegetation on the bush side. 'Forms a nice little cul-de-sac. Sean and I camped there once. God, what a time.'

'Jerra.'

That look had come on his face, the look he got when the past had hold of him. She knew he kept the deepest, the most important things to himself, but there was no end of surface stuff – names and places and anecdotes of boyish adventures – that began to drive her mad.

'The ranger never found us tucked away there. We used to sneak back up the road at night and pinch a hot shower from the caravan park—'

'Don't, Jerra.' Not today. It's Christmas. There's things ahead.

'What?' He looked at her, annoyed.

'That nostalgia stuff. Don't.'

'Why not, for God's sake?' His face hardened. He seemed ready to fight her on it this time.

'Because—'

'Because you weren't there. I'm excluding you when I remember. I'm sorry.' He slapped his arm and held up the crushed body of a march fly.

'No, because it makes you pathetic. You do it like an old man who can't handle the present.'

She gripped the handles of Sam's pusher and strode out. He opened his mouth but she spoke first. 'It makes me despise you.'

Labouring up the final hill in the windless hollow where cicadas belted out their unified note, she felt him lagging behind. He didn't seem to have any resistance left. You can follow, she thought; you can bloody well follow.

At the crest the salty breeze met Rachel full in the face, and at the sight of the sea, something rose in her.

'I'm gonna cut my hair off,' she said when Jerra came up alongside.

He looked at her, then down at the sea which he seemed to behold with relief. That feeling in her, yes, it was triumph. She had pushed down walls to live, to give life. She had been where there was no dependence, only a battle of solitary forces. And she had survived. After twenty years of confirming her own ineptitude, Rachel found she was strong. Never before had she felt such strength. Sweat cooled on her. She touched the welts on Jerra's shoulder. In her ocean of new feeling she knew she had to be the strong one.

'Yeah,' Jerra said, apprehending her again, 'me too.'

3

The whole car stank of sweat and cooked upholstery. Sam grizzled and squirmed in his seat. On the passenger's side, Jerra sat low with his head tilted back and the wind in his stubble. Rachel drove. They'd agreed on it. Everything they owned was stuffed into the old Holden; it was all of them driving back through the city, and neither heat nor traffic could stifle Rachel's spirit. This was her return. Every movement, every driving action was laden with purpose.

'Oh, Jesus.' Jerra sat straight in his seat as though something had bitten him.

The river was flat. They passed the old brewery. It wasn't far to Jerra's parents' place.

'Don't worry.' She reached over to touch the bristled surface of his head. 'It's only for a couple of weeks. We'll find a flat.'

'No. It's something else.'

Rachel drew in breath and held the wheel. 'Don't spoil this for me.'

'Hey, listen—'

'Something's happening for me, Jerra. I'm getting somewhere. Don't stuff it up.' She saw him stay stiff upright in the corner of her eye.

Sam cried and struggled. They rolled through Jerra's old neighbourhood, found the street in silence.

Pulling into the driveway, Rachel looked up at the big red house behind the silky oaks and saw Mrs Nilsam at the window. She wasn't waving. She looked quickly at Jerra, and then she got out and galloped up to the shady porch where the old woman stood, swollen-eyed and shaky. Rachel hugged her fearfully and spoke into that big, tanned neck.

'What's happened? Is Mr Nilsam all right?'

'Rachel. Oh, your hair – it's lovely.'

Rachel stood back and looked into the old woman's handsome face and then followed her down to the car where Jerra was unstrapping Sam. She felt herself go tight inside.

Jerra passed the child to his mother who touched him hungrily.

'It's Sean, isn't it?'

'In a car. Yesterday.'

'Funny. Back up the road, I knew.' He looked at Rachel with a sick smile and shrugged. 'I knew.'

Rachel looked down at him and a chink of panic opened in her. She felt Mrs Nilsam take her hand and squeeze it. There was strength there.

From the house, a faint call.

'That's your father. He's crook.'

Jerra looked up.

'One day, Sam,' the old woman said, holding the child up in the light, 'you and your kind'll have to carry yourself.'

Sam looked at her and bared his teeth.

Holding

for Derek

Hart sat back and listened to them speaking quietly in front. The station-wagon floated through the night streets towards the inner city, and Hart felt warm and fed and happier than he had been. Jan sat low in the passenger's seat. Clive drove. Clive was Hart's best friend. He was ten years older than Hart, and he still seemed like odd company to keep. Clive was like a friendly alien. He managed several companies, had a passion for technology, and he owned more credit cards than seemed necessary. He belonged to the Liberal Party, and to compound Hart's mystification, he was also a Protestant Christian. But for all that, Clive Genders was the most generous, compassionate man Hart had ever known, someone who wasn't afraid to admit ignorance or weakness. His laugh was warm and settling; he had a penchant for the scatological; he was always more than the sum of the things he stood for. To a man like Hart who worked with social workers and psychologists, Clive Genders was worth holding on to.

Hart watched them from the back seat. He'd been thinking about tonight's news footage from South Africa. A black mob. A woman in flames. It was soothing to watch the two little Genders boys beside him on the back seat asleep in an embrace. He pulled the blanket gently around them and heard Clive guffaw.

'Oh, tell 'em to shove it up their arse!'

'Oh, Clive.'

'I mean in a loving way, of course.' He laughed. 'Bloody bureaucrats.'

Tonight they'd drunk wine from 'the private collection', the Margaret River reds Clive kept in the grease-pit of the family garage. He was a man with good taste and no class.

'Don't be a twit, Clive.' Jan's dark face was greenish in the light of the old dash panel. Hart found her difficult; he never let on to Clive. She had a strangely downturned mouth which always made her seem disgruntled. Hart looked away, realizing he'd been observing her all evening. That mouth was so damned irritating, but, in a way, watchable.

'Send 'em a telegram: GET STUFFED, RUDE LETTER FOLLOWING.'

Hart laughed.

'Don't encourage him,' Jan said, softening a little, 'he's done it before.'

They reached Hart's street and sailed in to the kerb. He slid across the seat to the door and squeezed Clive's shoulder. He didn't flinch like he used to. As he turned in his seat, Clive's meaty face and receding hairline were illuminated in the light of the streetlamp. The boys called his baldness 'Daddy's growing forehead'.

'See you Friday, eh?'

'Care of the Magic Plastic,' said Clive.

'The teddy bears' picnic,' Jan said with that rich mouth of hers down at the corners. Her teeth were perfect.

'Thanks for dinner, Jan.'

'See you, Hart.'

'See you, Bleeder.'

Hart got out into the cold. The engine ran in the still street.

'Picnicks, Friday.' Clive worked the clutch.

The car's tail lights shrank away. Hart stood alone in the street with his breath hanging before him. The sky was clear. Dew glittered on the grass verge. Hart decided to walk. On nights like this, after fights especially, Andrea and he had always walked. She used to say it was cleansing. In his mind's eye he saw the shadow between Jan's lips. He needed a walk. The cold night scoured him.

A telephone ringing. He swam up, floated across to where it shook spastically on the wall. Took up the receiver. He heard a calm, authoritative voice. 'I am obliged to tell you that your friend Janice Genders has died as a result of a miscarriage. Goodbye.'

Hart sat up, awake. A dream. He felt bad, sick. A dream. He got up and drank some water. People didn't die from miscarriages any more, he thought. Besides, she's not even pregnant; they don't want any more kids. If I trusted any of the bastards I'd ask one of the psychs from work what it could mean. He'd never dreamt like that before. It scared him.

Before long he slept again, but in the morning, and for many mornings thereafter, he remembered that cold, administrative voice.

*

At work on Thursday, Hart admitted to the Unit a small boy whose eyes were like cinders. The boy looked at everything as though trying to will it away. Hart read his report and kept up a friendly, confident smile. The boy's parents seemed fastidious and bossy and suspicious; they seemed ashamed to be in such an institution. They kissed the boy and left without much reluctance. Walking down the corridor with that little boy, reading the awful case history as he went, Hart felt grateful that Andrea and he had never had children. Every day he saw these victims of carelessness and neglect and abuse. He and Andrea, he realized, in their clutching unhappiness, could have maimed children as easily as they'd maimed each other. He supposed it was something to be grateful for.

Clive strode into Picnicks burring the wad of credit cards in his fist. Hart was already at the table.

'Put 'em away, you don't fool me.'

'Just to remind you of the company you keep,' Clive said with a grin. 'How's the Bleeding Hart?'

'Fair.'

'Come on, old son. Fair? On Friday? What's wrong, is the *National Times* late on the stands, or something? It's Friday lunch. Picnicks!'

'And the Protestant deity's in his heaven.'

Clive's eyebrows went up the way they did when he was hurt. Hart squirmed. There was an unspoken agreement they had about humourless jibes. He felt muddled.

Just then Nick brought menus and friendly talk to their table by the window. Cars rolled past down Oxford Street. With his old gesture of boyish expectancy, Clive lay both hands flat on the inky-green linen. His new beard suited him, balanced his face, hid the strain of work. Nick told them the day's specials, joked with them as always, and Hart lightened a little at the sight of Clive's eagerness. The business of being here at Picnicks with him, ordering food and drink, distracted him from a creeping panic.

'It's still the best place, you know,' Hart said. He felt his face break in a grin. 'Look at it all, the china, the menu, the wine list. There's nothing like . . .'

Clive flounced his hands about. 'The ambience . . . the sweet ambience.' And they fell into laughter.

'Put those bloody credit cards away,' Hart said when they had quieted down. 'That one's a parking token, for God's sake, and this one, is this for opening other people's hotel doors?'

'Just a simple man with a simple man's capitalist foibles.'

Their bottle of Rosemount came. It lay awhile, sweating in its bucket of ice.

Clive's face straightened out. 'You look tired, mate. How's work?'

'Rough. The whole Unit's in chaos. We admitted this kid yesterday who prolapses his anus at will. No one knows what the hell to do. Medical staff gave up, that's why we've got him.'

'He does what?'

'He sits in a corner and pushes so hard his arse turns inside-out. After meeting his parents, pushing arse doesn't seem such a silly thing to do.'

Clive winced. 'Parenthood.'

'Oh, don't worry, you do all right, you and Jan.'

'Actually,' Clive said, eyes narrowing, 'Jamie has this habit of sticking his finger up his bum during his bedtime prayers. Gives him a rather contemplative look, really. Should I worry?'

'I'm a nurse, mate, not a theologian.'

They poured their wine and sat watching the traffic pass. It was peaceful here away from all that hopeless tangle.

'Speaking of theology, I rang a black clergyman today,' Clive said.

'Oh? Where's he from?' Hart watched a woman ride by with a laundry basket on her back.

'South Africa.'

'What?'

'Yeah.' Clive grinned. 'I rang Bishop Desmond Tutu. Toots to his friends.'

'Bullshit.'

'I did, I really did. We had a good old chat.'

'What, for your Tory mates?'

'Cynic! No, for myself. I asked him a few naïve questions. He was late for a dinner appointment. I taped it for you. Just to show you I've got a social conscience.'

'What'd he say?'

'Pray. And get ready to pick up the pieces.'

Their entrée arrived. Hart picked at his terrine; it was perfect but his appetite was leaving him. Clive ate and drank, and Hart felt him watching. Hart could feel himself sinking. Hold on to this, he told himself; this is good, this man, this food, this day; hold on.

'Another announcement,' Clive said.

'Let's hope it's good news.'

'Unexpected, but good. Jan's pregnant again.'

Hart felt the shock drop in him like a stone in a well. 'Oh.'

'Three months gone.'

'Are you sure?'

'A doctor told her. Technology told him. You know my weakness for technology.'

'Congratulations.' Hart saw the puzzlement on his friend's face. He ordered another bottle of Chardonnay. The meal was beautiful, dreamlike, graceful, but Hart felt disabled. He was unequal to it. Clive and he talked on, moving from children back to politics, on to their mutual hatred of football, then back to children, but Hart felt as though he was impersonating himself. He felt himself slipping. He drank more; ordered another bottle to cover his strange feelings of grief and anxiety.

When they parted just before three, Hart was drunk. He left Clive bemused in the car park and walked home along Oxford Street to sleep up for the evening shift. He thought about that voice in the dream. Yes, it was the voice of a public servant, a hospital administrator. Contempt soothed him for a moment. Bloody dreams. The thought came to him: What if she did die? What then?

During the next week Hart spent hopeless hours with the little boy they called The Pusher. Too much time, he knew. But it seemed desperately necessary to break into that ten-year-old before the case conference at the end of the week. Hart was agitated by the idea of this child at the mercy of the psychs and their useless academic curiosity. Hart wanted him out, better, gone. He knew he was panicking; it was as unprofessional as hell and he didn't care. Coming across The Pusher alone in a corner, pushing till his eyeballs surged, Hart whispered, 'What, you trying to move the fucking world?'

He gave himself till the end of the week before he'd sign himself off. He was losing it. He was lost.

When he woke in the afternoons, the house was big and empty. After all this time it was still hollow without Andrea, and now he wondered whether he mightn't have lost himself as well. He watched TV. There he was, every evening, that little black priest at the head of a snaking mob with the white soldiers looking on from their armoured cars. *There* was a man who'd found himself, he thought.

On Tuesday he saw a woman in the street whom he mistook for Jan Genders. He called out to her and when she turned around he saw it was a stranger, a woman with a small bright mouth and green eyes. He wasn't so much embarrassed as angry. He felt robbed. His fury did not abate. On TV that nervous little black man stood with his mouth open in the rising dust.

On Friday morning, Clive rang to cancel lunch at Picnicks.

'The old girl's a bit off colour. Think I'll go home and have lunch with her.'

Hart rang the Genders home.

'I heard you're a bit crook,' he said.

'Hart?'

'Yeah.'

'I'm having what you call a suspected miscarriage.'

'Oh, God.'

'You don't believe in Him, leave Him the hell out of it.'

'Do you?'

'When I can.'

'I had a dream.' Jesus, he was desperate. But for what?

'Martin Luther King.'

'What?' What? What? God, he was gonna burst into tears any minute.

'Forget it, boy. Clive isn't home.'

'I . . .'

'The doctor says I probably won't lose it.'

'Clive believes in doctors.'

'The doctor told me to stay in bed.'

'Oh. Sorry.'

She rang off. He stood there, hot, breathless. He went for a walk.

Across the road from Picnicks in a greasy little pinball joint, he ate a hamburger. He could see the flashing neon sign and the table in the window where he and Clive always sat. He was filled with self-contempt; he felt like a waif with his nose against the glass.

Home again, he rang off sick. He couldn't work. He couldn't force it any more. The case conference would be in progress now; the psychs would be devising a neat theory; The Pusher would be turning his arse out in a corner. Opening his fists by force of will, Hart said out loud: 'I am not coping.'

The weekend came and Hart stayed in the cold house. He took out the cassette Clive had given him and played it over and over.

My friend there is terrible violence to come, but we must resist. There is no choice for us. There is no choice for me. Pray for us. If you can do nothing else, pray . . .

On Saturday afternoon Hart walked down to the local pub on the corner. Its walls were adorned with smoke-stained fishing trophies, a turtle shell and a jumbo crayfish, the tail of which had fallen off years ago. Andrea and he had decided here one afternoon to get married. They were back two years later arguing the terms of separation. Hart drank in tempo with that horrible slipping feeling. The foul cloud of smoke and talk and memories pressed in. She'll lose that baby, he thought; and I feel guilty already, like it's something to do with me. Me! He drank up. To hell with them.

Following his feet up the hill, he thought about that dream. What was it supposed to be, the voice of God, for Chrissake? Yeah, Clive's little Protestant deity. Yeah, I can see him as a bloody hospital administrator.

In the night he was woken by another dream. In it, Bishop Desmond Tutu led an endless procession like those he'd seen on TV. Funerals, mass funerals. There was dust and chants and black hands and pink upturned palms. As the crowd drew near he saw the coffins. There they were, atop the long, sealed boxes, the white bodies of people he knew. Andrea, Jan (so white), Clive, The Pusher. In his dream Hart leapt down from an armoured car, bashed through the cordon, and ran out on to the dusty road. The small, robed black man, spectacles glinting, paced with shoulders down. Hart ran towards him, but the bishop held a hand up to him, signalling him to keep away. Dust was everywhere like incense. That pink palm turned against him.

He was awake. His head throbbed.

Sunday evening the phone rang out in the cold house. It seemed about right to Hart. He answered.

'She lost it.'

'Oh, Clive.'

'She's all right. They say it was dead for a week anyway.'

'Was it . . . hard going for her?'

'Fucking awful. Worse than having a live one.'

'Were you there?'

'Of course I was. Oh, God.' Clive sighed; it was a dead sound.

'You all right?'

'She wants to come to Picnicks on Friday. All right with you? Wants to break a few traditions.'

Hart stiffened. 'Sure.'

'I know you find her a pain in the arse.'

'No, that's not true.' He looked out of the window and saw the lights of the city. He was lost. 'Christ, it's all so bloody futile, isn't it?'

'No, just a little complicated. Not futile.'

Hart sighed. 'The little Protestant deity, eh?'

'Ah, you see? We'll make a spiritual giant of you yet.'

Hart listened. He heard Clive pause as though swallowing something. He heard him sniff. And then, down the line, out of the hollow night, Hart heard him laugh. It was strong. It was rich. With the lights of the city presenting themselves dumbly to him, Hart felt his whole being straining, holding on to that sound.

More

1

He pauses at the door and wonders about lipstick. The house is in darkness. He breathes through his teeth, feeds the key in, opens the door. In the bathroom he strips and he stuffs his clothes deep into the laundry basket. He crushes them down. The mirror shows him his white face. On the kitchen table, held down by an apple, there is a note. *Gave up waiting*. He creeps to the bedroom. Streetlight divides the bed. Two figures jack-knife across it, one large, one small. He eases out. Down the hall he folds into the little bed with the Mickey Mouse quilt. Mobiles hang from the ceiling. He switches the light out, but he senses the shiny bright things turning in the dark above and his heart won't ease up. He puts the nightlight on again and looks up at the mobiles: fish floating on some hidden draught. He gets out of bed and goes to the little wardrobe. On it there is a photograph in a Perspex frame. It shows a blood-spattered, unshaven, mad-eyed young man looking into a humid crib which holds a baby. The baby is big and battered-seeming. The young man in the picture looks hungry for it. He takes the paper from the frame and holds it up to the nightlight. He watches for movement, but all that moves is his heart in his chest, butting blindly against itself. And he sleeps. The bed smells of his son. He feels himself sink into that sweet Johnson & Johnson smell, knowing, even as he swims into sweetness with fish flying above, that everything is not all right.

The weekend before Rachel's exams, they drove north to Guilderton for the weekend. The evening air was full of the smell of coming heat. In the warm night on the veranda they played their mongrel game of chess. Jerra liked a skirmish. He didn't care so much for victory; he just liked to mow a path now and then, to see pieces fall. Rachel told him he had the tactics of a blind bull. She was reading Hemingway. He nodded. He wanted to ask her how she was liking Hemingway, but he just made his moves and watched the streaks of smoke from the mosquito coils. Now and then, the flash of the lighthouse broke the night. He drank too much beer. He lost the game and followed her to bed.

'**Hope no one** turns up,' Rachel said in the darkness a moment before he was finally asleep. The curtains lit up a second before leaving them again in darkness.

'Who?' he asked, after a pause.

'Our friends. Anyone. I want some peace.'

'And quiet. Don't tell me, I know.'

'It's just the exams, and everything. I'm going mad.'

'Yeah.' Assignments, essays, exams, textbooks. God, he was sick of it. 'No one'll turn up.'

'I hope not.'

'Blame me if they do,' he said.

'Why?'

'I'm unlucky.'

In the night, Sam woke and he cried for two hours and ten minutes. He kicked and scratched and drooled as each of them tried to comfort him, and then they began shouting at each other and in the end Rachel wept.

'Why are you like this, Jerra?' she called, holding Sam away from him.

'Everything's gone to shit. Your misery is contagious.'

'Oh, you can't bear other people's sickness or unhappiness, can you? You can't tolerate it.'

Sam ceased wailing and fell abruptly to sleep.

'I know,' said Jerra, lowering his voice. 'I'm not patient enough.'

'Not mature enough.'

'Don't social work me, for Chrissake. OK, I know. That's how I got into this mess. I was too young. I was stupid.'

'Thank you.'

'Thank *you*.'

Jerra prepared himself for more sobbing, but she climbed into bed with Sam and left him there. He stood for a while outside the door. There was excitement in cruelty, and the idea of it burnt him.

At the bend in the river, before it deepened off against the bar sealing its mouth, there was clean, shallow water and shade in the lee of the limestone bluff. Sam sat astride Rachel's brown belly and splashed. A gull shadow passed over them.

'Burr-burr!' Sam yelled.

'Bird,' said Rachel.

'Bird,' said Jerra, wishing she would turn her head and meet his eyes with a smile.

He lay back in the water, shifting on the tide-ribbed bottom, until only his mouth and nose were above the surface, and with his eyes open he saw the sky through a shifting filter of river water. He stayed there. He remembered a night when the colicky sawing of baby screams pierced him finally and truly, when he tore Sam from his neck and held him out and shook him till his head might come away. It was in the moment before slamming his little body into the wall that he lay him on the bed and went outside into the scathing forest cold. The crying stopped suddenly, and he thought he'd killed him. Rachel was too sick to know. And Jerra stood alone out there with the God-like silence towering at him. He knew then that he was capable of the darkest things.

Jerra lurched upright, sputtering.

'Allo,' Sam said.

'Hello, mate.'

Rachel made no comment as he went off on his own in the afternoon when heat was fattening the air. He took a flick rod and a knife and bucket. The sun glowered and stung his skin. From a rock in a deep bend of the river, he fished for bream using worms and a small amount of lead. He stubbed a toe and lost a rig. Two little girls joined him, and they fished like experts. They giggled when he begged tackle off them. One of them caught a gobbleguts. Jerra then lost a second rig and was too embarrassed to ask again, so he left them to themselves. As he walked away, it occurred to him that they thought he was an old man. A funny old man. He was twenty-four years old.

Sam and Rachel lay asleep in the hot little beach house. He sat and waited, listened to his blood.

At dusk, cutting lemons for the salad, Jerra saw the knife-steel sink into his finger.

'Shit. I'm cut.' He began to dance. 'It's bad.' He stopped. There was blood on the linoleum. He went back to the sink. For a moment, in the madness of shock, it occurred to him that he might have cut the whole finger off, and he began to shift the gore-smeared dishes about, looking for his fingertip. But then Rachel grabbed his hand and lashed a teatowel to his finger. The kookaburra prints on the linen began to blush.

At the first-aid station beside the shop and garage, the little man told him the wound would need sutures.

'It's a biggun,' he said. 'Probably sev-eared the nerves.'

Jerra watched him wrap it in a constrictive bandage, and was disturbed by the grease on the man's hands. He'd never been ministered to by a mechanic.

'Have to get a doctor on to that. Gingin's the closest town. Do it in the morning, unless you're worried.'

Rachel looked at him. 'You worried?'

Jerra shrugged.

'Well, I'm not worried,' she told the man.

All night Jerra lay with his hand throbbing. Sunburn caused his skin to feel as though it was shrinking on him.

He saw oily limbs and the twist of momentum. His head in the cradle of her pelvis. Smelled the pungent shifts in her. He saw. He saw. He saw that she was not Rachel.

*

At dawn he woke and wondered how he could possibly move, get up, get out of bed and go on. He felt like the maze was closing on him.

Hot wind blew through the car on the way back from the doctor's. His finger was tight with numbness and through it he swore he could feel the sutures moving. His back stung. He winced at every bump in the road.

'I know about it, Jerra.'

It wrenched him around in his seat. 'About what?'

'Quiet, you'll wake Sam.'

'Know *what*?' he murmured.

She drove. He shored himself against her tears, but she just drove and nothing came.

They'd been back ten minutes when Rachel came running into the kitchen. Jerra braced himself.

'Sam's eaten Ratsak!'

He wilted with relief.

'Poison, Jerra!'

Sam smiled. His white hair stood at odds with itself. There was a rime of green around his mouth. Jerra seized him and took him to the sink. He prised open his mouth with a finger. Sam giggled. Jerra reached into the tiny throat. The giggle choked off into a cry of alarm. Jerra felt the teeth set into the flesh of his good hand.

'Start the car.'

'Who the hell'd leave rat poison around for kids to get into?' Jerra muttered in the surgery. He paced around the doctor who held Sam over a bowl. Vile black stuff was coming up. Sam bellowed and gagged.

'Dave and Debbie don't have kids,' Rachel said. 'They wouldn't have to think about it. It's not their fault.'

'Should have kept an eye—'

'Oh, leave off, Jerra.'

'Well, you'd think—'

'What?'

'It just shouldn't have happened.'

'Yeah, well lots of things happen that should never happen.'

The look he got from her sent him to the back of the room where light filtered down clean from a skylight. He stood there, thinking of something to say.

'Skylight'd save your money, Doc.'

The doctor looked at him, brow askew, and went back to the business of helping Sam vomit. 'There's no sign of anything,' he said. 'Probably just had it on his lips.'

'Christ.'

Rachel began packing as soon as they got back to the beach house.

'It's not working out,' she said.

Jerra could not fathom her control.

'No, it's a disaster, eh.'

She fell on the bed and hid her face from him.

Jerra went outside and watched crickets leap out of the lawn to escape Sam's trundling manoeuvres on the plastic trike.

On the highway heading back, he leans across to where she sits rigid at the wheel.

'Look—'

'Don't, you'll kill me.'

He opens his mouth again but she cuts him off.

'There's too much on my plate, Jerra. I can't know about it, I can't listen to you tell me how sorry you are or aren't. I have to pass these exams. There's no way I can live if I fail them. I have to not go mad. OK, melodrama, violins, I know.'

'OK.'

'It happens, Jerra.'

'It's over, it didn't even start.'

Sam sleeps between them, drooling and awry in his little seat.

A hard, tiny sound comes out of Rachel's throat. She pulls over and begins to take in long breaths.

'Look, I can't go home, just now,' she says.

'Wanna go back?'

'No.'

'Want me to drive?'

She shakes her head. 'I need to be with someone. Away.'

Jerra sits. The blue, dry land goes away from him in all directions. He sighs. 'Mum and Dad are down at the Cut. You mean them, don't you?'

She starts the car.

'It's a hell of a drive from here,' he says.

She gets into top gear and good posture and he sits back with his eyes closed.

2

It was dark when they rolled into the peppermint clearing, and in front of the timber cabin a fire sent sprays of sparks into the night. The smells of rivermud and peppermint and boiling crabs met them as they got out, and Sam finally stopped crying.

'It's Jerra, Tom!'

The silhouette of Jerra's mother came from behind the steaming old copper and met them in the dark.

'Spare a bed?' he asked as she smote him with kisses.

His mother turned and bellowed back into the house. 'They're staying, Tom! Put some beer in the fridge! You've cut yourself. And oh!' She gathered Sam up and touched his tousled hair which seemed to glow in the dark. 'What brings you down here to your old Granma, Sam?'

'Disaster,' said Rachel.

'Unrelieved misfortune,' Jerra said, and to his surprise, they each managed a laugh. Backlit in the doorway, he saw the reduced outline of his father. He looked worse.

Piles of rivercrabs, red and steaming, covered the table spread with newspapers and battered china plates and bowls of brown vinegar. There was fresh white bread, mustard, beer and chilli sauce, and as they ate and broke and sucked, dunked, smeared, cursed, Jerra watched as though he were not quite present. On Rachel's knee, a revived Sam sucked the sweet, white flesh from crablegs. He reared and laughed his little screech at the sight of his grandfather with a claw on his nose like a clothespeg. The old man looked happy, even though the cancer had him for good now. Jerra watched his mother. Her tan made her leathery and easy to look at. She had broadened these past years and she seemed to have grown stronger. She took more of every kind of space. Right there in her balding armchair at table, she looked happily immovable and he was filled with affection for her. He watched them all around this florid mess of crabs, the room full of eating noise and baby talk. His family, his blood. Oh, God, it burned fierce in him tonight, the desire to serve to protect to be loyal unto death. No room for irony tonight, and the feeling grew in him, fattened and rose like bread in his chest until he threw down his fork and left the table.

Out in the smoky dark he found the outhouse and locked himself in and waited. Sooner or later, he told himself, in a while it won't seem so important. Perspective. Irony. Sense. But he waited in vain.

Late in the night, when the others were asleep inside, Jerra played his father a song on the guitar. The lamp hissed. Mosquitoes pressed the wire all around the veranda. There was a melancholic pleasure in picking out the simple melody. He felt the strings emboss his fingertips, the vibration against his chest. He picked clumsily, handicapped by the gauze on his finger.

'What'll you do when you get famous?' his father asked, pulling a blanket over his knees in the silence that remained.

'I'll never get famous, Dad. I just wanna get old.'

'Yeah, boy, so did I.'

Jerra bit.

'Would you leave Perth?' his father said without pause.

'Oh, I'd miss the sun.'

'There's sun all over the world, they tell me.'

Jerra laughed. Always the same game. When Jerra gets famous. He wondered whether it was a way for the old man to stave off disappointment.

'You weren't moping about me out there, were you?'

He looked into his father's dark, dry eyes and saw something new.

'I was chucking up. Must've eaten something.'

'I taught you never to lie.'

Jerra found a chord and sang.

'It's a sin to tell a lie . . .'

The old man looked away out into the dark and Jerra felt the chord die against his chest.

'No, not about you, Dad. I can't even believe *that* yet. No, it won't beat you. You won't die.' He rested his chin against the smooth wood of the sound box. 'No. I s'pose it sounds weird, but in there tonight I felt sort of . . . unworthy.'

'Was it us?'

'Me.' Jerra tried to laugh. 'Jesus, it's guilt!' Any moment now he was going to blurt it all out like a child. He ached to confess every kind of betrayal.

'Things you don't know about.'

'Rachel and Sam. You belong to them.'

'Sometimes I feel like pissing off like I used to. I haven't measured up, have I?'

'You've done orright, Jerra. You grew up through some rough business. You're not too proud yet to be guilty. And you've had your losses.'

'Yeah,' Jerra said, full of bitterness. 'I've seen a few buried.'

'You worry about the living. Like your mother says: don't be bitter, be better.'

'Want me to take you out in the boat tomorrow?'

'What – for a last ride?'

'Geez, Dad,' he winced, 'be better, for Godsake.'

'Play "Danny Boy".'

Jerra picked it out, best he could.

When his father got up to go in to bed a while later, he kissed Jerra's brow and touched the guitar.

'When a bloke finds out how long he's got left, he knows there's more to it, son. Stupid thing is, there's always been more.'

Alone, Jerra listened to the mosquitoes. He sat on his father's reading chair. Frogs began to change pitch. A waterbird slapped away somewhere out on the estuary. He fidgeted with the small pile of books on the chair-arm. Beneath a volume of bush ballads he found *The Book of Common Prayer* and he lifted it in surprise.

Morning light lay on the water. The boat turned at anchor. In the bow, the old man sat mixing pollard. Jerra saw the lines in his face and knew he was in pain.

'Takes you back.'

His father scattered moist grains across the water. Jerra cast a line out and heard the sinker pop the surface.

'Remember the pelican caught out here in the net? Years ago.'

The old man shook his head. His face was hard-set.

'There were things I wanted to say that day, Dad.'

'Boy. I need to lie down.'

Jerra felt the chill on his father's face. 'I'll take you back.'

As he hauled anchor rope across the gunwale, the boat turned lamely in whatever direction resistance lay.

In the twilight before dark, Jerra and Rachel left Sam with his grandparents and went walking. The air was warm but the mosquitoes were not out yet and sounds of the bush were muted. They walked on a soft clay path between blackbutts. Bracken rose at the base of the trees. The ground felt damp and sunken. When the path was wide enough they walked abreast. In the narrow sections Jerra took the lead and held out a hand to fend off spiderwebs. For a long time neither spoke. Jerra felt the callouses on his fingertips. They tasted brassy in his mouth. He looked at the ugly sutures in his index finger.

'I s'pose your mum and dad walk down here a lot.'

'Used to. Mum still does, I s'pose.'

'I like her. I like them both.'

'Yeah, I know.'

'We could turn out like that if we tried.'

Like what, he thought. Old and dying? But he checked himself. Try. Be better not bitter.

'Yeah I guess there's worse ways to turn out.'

'How is it with your dad?'

'We talked.'

'Did you know he prays?'

'How did you know?'

'He told me. He was frightened to tell you. You must have jumped down his throat when you were younger.'

Jerra felt bracken sliding across his flanks. He smelt her near him. He reached and touched her and they stopped walking.

'Yeah. I did. I didn't understand.'

'What about now? Do you understand now?'

'Not really. Maybe you need to be dying to understand.'

'Your dad said we were always dying. He's pretty wise, in his way.'

'Gee, you two are as thick as thieves.' He felt her flesh cool beneath his palms. 'I'm not dying. I'm living.'

Half-way across the distance between them as he leant out to kiss her, the undergrowth exploded and shadows showered up in every direction.

He cried out in fear.

'Quail,' Rachel said.

In the silence he heard the blood beating at his throat.

Death belongs to the dead, his father told him, and sadness to the sad

1

When junkies came into his café to nod and mutter and make cloths of themselves on his tables, The Man knew he was looking upon death itself. But he served them because when he was a boy in Naples he had learnt to walk straight and not look over his shoulder. Death belongs to the dead, his father told him, and sadness to the sad. On this street, far from Naples, there was death, there was sadness, and he did not look over his shoulder. He served the dead, took their money, and walked straight.

But the street and the café were not without happiness. In the afternoons people sat in the bookshop down the road and gossiped as they flicked through books they could not afford, while their children made their faces hideous against the plate glass to shock passers-by. Old men on the stoops smoked and called to one another in strange tongues. Drunks woke beneath the Moreton Bay figs in the park to discover that death had not claimed them in the night. Taxi drivers double-parked to complain and shake their heads in contentment before the peak hour. And in the evenings, before the café was full, the old pub on the corner was jammed with young people and the roar of music from a band whose guitarist wandered out to play twenty-minute solos to strollers-by. Cars slowed up to listen. People stepped over the long cord that trailed him; they smiled and were confused. Detectives came every night to get him off the street, but they did not beat him up, and when they were gone he would hang out the window to shoot riffs into moving cars.

During the mornings, though, there was mostly sadness. The street was forlorn and the junkies came into the café, and there were people with hangovers or marriage problems or people who seemed worried about how they looked. It was in the mornings that the Dying Gentleman began to come in.

Each day the Dying Gentleman sat by the window and looked hungrily out at the passing traffic. He sat with his hat on the table and his brogues flat on the floor, and sometimes a thin beam of winter sun would give his head a tonsure. At first, The Man, who knew a hungry person when he saw one, offered him the breakfast menu, but the newcomer shook his head and asked for a cold glass of milk. His lips barely moved. The Man listened: it was the voice of death. He got the Dying Gentleman his milk and heard the voice of death thank him.

It soothes my stomach, the Dying Gentleman said. He put a white hand on his belly and moved it across. He had never been handsome, The Man guessed, but you could see he had once been young and vital. He was wasting. It looked like cancer. The Man took his money and did not look over his shoulder.

But in time, The Man found himself unable to resist the sight of the Dying Gentleman. From behind the coffee machine, he watched surreptitiously. Each morning, the Dying Gentleman came in looking a little more hollow, a shade whiter. The monkish spot the ascending sun made on the top of his head seemed more luminous every day.

How is the stomach today? he began to ask the Dying Gentleman as he brought his glass of milk. The Dying Gentleman shook his head and drank. He looked as though he was starving, but as though a meal would murder him.

2

One evening, a man came running into the café with blood issuing from great wounds in his face. His jacket was torn and a swamp of blood rose from his armpit.

Someone is after me! he screamed. The Man took him by the bloody collar and put him out on the street and pushed him away along the pavement. He watched him stagger down towards the roar of music and leave a trail of blood. The Man saw him collide with detectives who had arrived to shoo the electric guitarist off the street. When he turned to go back to his café, he saw a thin, dark man holding a cleaver. He had a drooping moustache and he stood near the door, the cleaver at his side. The Man took a breath, walked straight past him and went into the café without looking back.

3

As the days became longer, the morning sun lay heavy on the Dying Gentleman who sat by the window with his milk. The light made him ghostly and The Man did not like to look.

The stomach? he would ask. The Dying Gentleman shook his head and put the hand to the belly. His flesh was translucent. Sad world, The Man said, despite himself. His customer shrugged and looked for a moment as though he might disagree. The Man left him with his milk.

It was Sunday morning when the Dying Gentleman came in and ordered bacon and eggs and sausages and short black coffee. The hot sun cut the café in half.

Feeling better? The Man asked.

Yes, the Dying Gentleman said. He put his hat on the table and straightened the little blue feather in the band, and The Man felt a happy twitch in his chest as he called the order through.

When he brought the breakfast, he saw the determination in the Dying Gentleman's features. From behind the coffee machine, he saw him eat all of it – the bacon, the eggs, the sausages, and the short black coffee – before putting his knife and fork down to watch the traffic pass. Then he got up and went to the pay phone by the door. The Man poured coffees and watched him dial. He saw the Gentleman straighten and speak and then return the piece to its cradle. He saw him put his hand to the window. He saw the black hole his mouth made and he got out from behind the counter and caught the Gentleman before he fell, and the wind escaping from his throat was like the gentle sound of passing traffic. The Man felt heat and there was a terrible stench. The Dying Gentleman's head was on his chest, his jacket was slipping up his arms.

Junkies nodded in the corner. The sun did not reach them. He looked down into the Gentleman's face and saw the black hole of his mouth. The darkness of it seemed to go for ever down.

The Man looked up and saw that people had stopped their talking and drinking, and as he held the body and felt it belong to him, he suddenly knew that Naples was on the other side of the world, that boyhood was further, and that death was a lifetime, a lunchtime, a breath away.

Blood and Water

Since it was the day of Preparation, in order to prevent the
bodies from remaining on the cross on the sabbath (for
that sabbath was a high day), the Jews asked Pilate that
their legs might be broken, and that they might be taken
away. So the soldiers came and broke the legs of the first,
and of the other who had been crucified with him; but
when they came to Jesus and saw that he was already dead,
they did not break his legs. But one of the soldiers pierced
his side with a spear, and at once there came out blood and
water.

John xix, 31–34

Rachel laughed and there was water down her leg.

'It's coming,' she said.

Jerra leapt up and switched the TV off. For a moment
they stood there and regarded the trails on her thighs. A car
accelerated up the hill and passed with a hiss outside. Rain
fell; the gutters were thick with it. They heard it chug in the
downpipes.

'This is gonna be the happiest night of my life,' he said.
He put on a record. Suddenly the house was full.

*

The midwife came, felt Rachel's abdomen, and commandeered their bed. Fires purred in the stove and the fireplace. The street was quiet. They played Haydn on the stereo and held hands during Rachel's contractions. They heard the midwife's snores. Her name was Annie. She was a tall, athletic woman who always wore her hair tied back in a scarf. She believed in God and healing and the goodness of people's bodies. Rachel and Jerra thought she was a little weird, but they had come to love her these past months. She was gentle. She warmed her hands. Her smile was reassuring.

In the light of the fire, Rachel's flesh looked polished. Jerra rubbed her back and whispered in her ear. She breathed across her contractions.

'It's fine,' she said. 'I can do it. Nice here. Look at the fire.'

The rushes came on like advancing weather. Jerra saw her knotting up till her flesh became armour and she hissed and they counted and Annie came out to sit by the fire.

'Having a baby?'

Rachel laughed. In the lull, Jerra sponged the sweat from her. She rested her head on his chest and closed her eyes. Her long braid fell across his thigh. He saw Annie by the fire. She too had her eyes closed and she was moving her lips. Praying, he thought; she's bloody praying. He remembered the prayer his mother had sung him at bedtime when he was a child, before it all got too embarrassing.

> *Gentle Jesus, meek and mild*
> *Look upon a little child*
> *Pity his simplicity*
> *Suffer him to come to Thee . . .*

Maybe I'll even sing it to this little critter, he thought; just out of nostalgia – what the hell.

At two o'clock the contractions took Rachel with such force that pauses between became moments of irony rather than serious relief. Jerra rubbed oil on her lips. He massaged the small of her back. He felt the vibrations in her flesh. He tried, he stayed close, he felt it in his skin, but he couldn't know it for himself; he couldn't know what it was like.

Annie gloved up for an internal.

'Having babies'd be fine,' Rachel panted, 'if it wasn't for other people's hands up you.' She winced, writhed a little.

'You're not dilating,' Annie said. 'You're so angry in there I can't feel it right. We've got twins, people, or a breech. How you feel?'

'Better when you. Get. Your. Hand. Out. Ah. I got plenty left.'

'Better call the doc. We might have to go to hozzie.'

'I need a crap.'

'Get the commode, Jerra.'

He heard his footsteps on the plastic-draped floor. It was like walking on water.

Jerra drove and the women sat in the back. Though he knew the way, he needed to be told. Annie shouted directions over his shoulder and comforted Rachel at the same time. He saw their moving shadows in the mirror. The hospital loomed. He had forgotten a jumper. He wished he hadn't worn overalls. They'll think we're hippies, he thought.

'Don't cry,' murmured Annie to Rachel. 'You got plenty left.'

They waited outside the emergency entrance. It was a private hospital. They had saved for insurance in case this should happen.

In the lift they propped Rachel up during contractions. At the desk they asked her to fill out a form. Jerra tried to be calm.

'I can only be an observer now,' Annie said. 'But the doc'll be here soon. Let's hold tight.'

Nurses and orderlies crowded round, strapping things on, tucking, adjusting. Someone cheerful inserted an intravenous drip.

'Try it at home, eh?'

'Be tough,' Annie whispered.

Jerra saw Rachel on her back on the bed. She breathed slow and deep in a trough.

'Let's just get this little fella out and go home,' she murmured.

It was five in the morning. At six their doctor came. He was a small man, a conservative dresser. He seemed to like people to think he was a conservative man as well, though it was just a front. Rachel liked him. She said he was old-style, that he didn't play God. She called him Doc.

'Four centimetres,' he said, wiping his glasses. 'Like trying to drive a bus through a gas-pipe.'

Jerra felt hyperventilated. He wished the big clock across the room could be covered somehow. He saw blisters of sweat bursting on Rachel's face.

'We're getting two heartbeats here,' someone said. The room seemed full of people.

'Can't we get a scan?' Jerra asked. 'We don't really know what we've got here.'

Someone mumbled something. Rachel let out a tiny yelp of pain.

'Time for an epidural,' someone said.

'I got plenty left,' said Rachel.

'Can't we get an ultra-sound?' Jerra asked.

A masked face tutted. 'All that technology. Dear, dear.'

'That's why we're here,' Jerra said quietly through his teeth. 'It's not for the warm feeling it gives us.'

'What do *you* think, Rachel?' the doc asked.

'Can't you send them all out?'

'It's their hospital.'

'I didn't want drugs.'

'Neither did I. But you're tired. You've worked hard enough for two babies already.'

Her face went white-hard. Jerra breathed through the contraction with her. He kept his face close to hers. They had trained for this and it worked. She beat the pain.

'I'll think about it,' she said in the short lull.

'I've got to get back for morning surgery. They'll call me about the scan. Be yourself.'

It went on all morning. Rachel whooped and hissed and panted and turned to ice only to melt and begin again. Breathing with her, Jerra was almost delirious. His head was gorged with oxygen. The clock was cruel with him. Rachel got older and older.

At nine someone wheeled a trolley in and inserted an

epidural into Rachel's spine. Jerra watched it happen as though he was absent from himself. 'We don't want drugs if it can be avoided,' he said to the white smock. 'We want to be reasonable—'

'This is a hospital,' the smock said.

At ten he paced the room alone. Annie was asleep down the hall on the floor of the fathers' room. Rachel had been wheeled out to the ultra-sound room and they'd stopped him going. I'm weak, he thought. I'm piss-weak. He paced like somebody on television and it didn't seem funny. He was almost jogging. He felt ill. He paced. He knew he'd die if he stopped. Outside, through the frosted glass, a day was happening; it was going on without him.

By the door of the delivery room he saw Rachel's candlewick gown hanging from a peg, and below, her sheepskin boots. He picked up the boots and squeezed them; he held the gown to his face, and in that moment it seemed possible that they might not bring her back. He stood out in the corridor. A nurse smiled at him. He felt something logging up behind his eyes. He ran to the toilet down the hall. On the toilet it felt as though his blood was running out of him. He was afraid.

He woke with his ear against the white wall. Sleep. He had been asleep. A few minutes? A moment?

The flush of the cistern sounded like a mob in a stadium. Out in the hall, a thread of that old tune stuck to him.

Gentle Jesus, meek and mild . . .

The delivery room was still empty. He paced in a wide arc from one corner to the other. His head ached. He began to jog. Fifteen hours. He wondered what he had been like fifteen hours ago.

Twenty minutes later a white crew wheeled Rachel in. They shepherded Jerra into a corner while they renewed her spinal block. Annie came in looking sick. He wanted to speak to her but he couldn't decide what to say. Instead he elbowed his way to the bed.

'Just one,' somebody said. 'Breech.'

'Will it fit?' he asked.

'Has to, now. Too late for a C-section.'

'You OK?' he whispered to Rachel.

She nodded. Her lips were dry. Her eyes had retreated. He found a flannel and squeezed some droplets on to her mouth. It was suddenly conceivable to him that she might die, that she was *able* to die. He lurched.

'Get him a chair.'

He heard Annie whisper in his ear from behind, 'They've brought in a gynie. Be brave.'

'Doctor O'Donelly will be down soon,' someone said, plugging in something.

'The Knife,' Annie muttered. 'Isn't there anyone else?'

'You don't work here any more, Annie.'

'I remember. But these people are paying for this. They're consumers. They have rights. Did the patient request or assent to the epidural? The IV? To be lying flat on her back?'

'I didn't consent to any fucking thing,' Rachel hissed. 'They're gonna do what they want.'

'Annie, I'm warning you,' a smock said.

'I want to squat,' Rachel breathed.

'You've got no legs.'

Jerra got down close to her. 'C'mon. We have to beat these fuckers. Let's breathe, c'mon, don't lose it, let's breathe.' He stayed close to her. He could not imagine what must be happening inside her; it was another universe beyond that hard-white flesh.

Shifts changed. Annie sat by Rachel, crooning and stroking, and he went to call his parents. They must know something's up, he thought. His mother wept. He wanted to throw up.

Breathing. Breathing. Walls bent. He was in a bellows. *Gentle Jesus, meek and mild, stop me going fucking wild . . .*
Eat, they told him.
Pant, they told him.
Die, they told him.
They told him.

The gumbooted gynaecologist strolled in at one after the pushing had begun.
'OK, let's get this job underway. She doing all right?'
'She's fine,' Rachel croaked. 'And. We been. Going. Eight. Een. Hours. Mis. Ter. Ummmmh.'
'Isn't she terrific?'
Jerra knew that all the hatred he had ever felt before was merely ill-will and mild dislike.
'Ten centimetres.'
Trolleys clattered. A ticking box appeared behind Rachel's head and someone connected it to the IV.
'I don't want syndemetrine.'

'You're tired, lovie.'

'And you're not me.'

Annie gave Jerra a defeated look. He whispered, 'Beat him, Rachel.' He saw she couldn't go on much longer. When she pushed, her veins rode up through her flesh.

There was a crowning of sorts. The perineum strained. Rachel's anus dilated like a rose opening. At each contraction something showed like a tongue at the mouth of her vagina. It was flesh. Then he saw black. Merconium.

'That's shit,' he said. 'It's in distress.'

'Are you a midwife?' someone asked.

'Testicles,' he said. 'God, it's a boy before it's a baby.'

At each contraction the raw, swollen testicles came out a little further, only to be strangled in the lull by the closing gap.

'I love you,' he said in her ear.

Someone sniffed. A crowd of smocks and masks. O'Donelly moved in. Somewhere Jerra saw the white face of their own doctor. He saw the scissors opening her up. He saw them cut from her vagina to anus. There was blood. There were great silver clamps pendulous from Rachel's flesh. Almost from within hers there was another little pair of buttocks.

'Push, Mrs Nilsam!'

'Legs up round his ears,' Annie said in his ear.

'Heartbeat faint now, Doctor.'

'OK, let's get him out.'

Rachel reared as hands went up inside her. Jerra saw blood and shit on a forearm. Rachel let out a cry and unleashed a foot from its stirrup. She kicked. A smock took the heel in the chest. She tried again, but hands took the foot and pinned it.

Now there were legs within legs.

'Jerra? Jerra?'

'Beat 'em, Rachel. Beat their arses off. At least you can shit and bleed on 'em.'

'No heartbeat.'

They were wrenching now, and twisting out the little arms and applying forceps to the aftercoming head.

'Jerra?'

'Oh, fuck me.'

A little puce head slipped out, followed by a rush of blood and water. Jerra saw it splash on to the gynaecologist's white boots. Across Rachel's chest the little body lay tethered for a moment while smocks and masks pressed hard up against Rachel's wound. He saw a needle sink in. Someone cut the cord. Blood, grey smears of vernix. The child's eyes were open. Jerra felt them upon him. From the little gaping mouth, pink froth issued. They snatched him up.

'Should have been a bloody caesar,' someone muttered.

Rachel groaned to get her breath while they sewed her.

Jerra saw the child hollow-chested on the trolley where the smocks sucked him out. He heard the deadly sound of it and he saw the gloved hands on the shiny little valves. With its blacksmeared hair, the baby's head looked like the dark side of the moon.

That's a dead baby, thought Jerra. That's it. She can't see it. How will I say it?

... suffer him to come to Thee ...

A chest flutter.

Oh, Jesus Christ, he thought. Gentle Jesus, don't play with me. Let him be dead but don't crucify me.

The chest filled.

Oh, don't fuck around with me!

A hand moved. Five fingers.

Oh dear God.

Other hands were gentle with it. There was grace in the plying of his limbs. A horrible ache rose from low in Jerra's spine. He knew it was love.

'Is he all right?' Rachel croaked. She licked her lips. 'Jerra?'

'They've got him.'

The paediatrician looked up. A little cough entered the room. Then another.

'He's crying,' Rachel said. 'I can't see him.'

They brought him over, wrapped in a blanket. In one nostril there was a clear plastic tube.

'On oxygen,' someone said.

Jerra hugged himself. 'Is he OK?'

'He'll need some help.'

Jerra felt those eyes on him. Blood and water bubbled out of the infant's mouth.

'Son of God,' Annie said.

'Grab that side of the trolley, Mr Nilsam. Let's get this boy down to ICU.'

As he ran out with the smocks, Jerra saw that the room was empty of white figures and only Rachel and Annie were left behind. They were holding each other.

Corridors, doors, potted palms. Past them, Jerra ran. People blurred by but he saw those black eyes on him and he wondered who he was a day ago.

*

The little boy held his hand and bleated up fluid as the paediatrician inserted a tube into the raw-cut navel. Jerra's eyes stung with tears.

'What's his chances? No bullshit. Please don't lie to me.'

The paediatrician looked up from his task. Only his eyes were visible, but he seemed to Jerra to be more than a technician. 'Not bad, I'd say. Then again, I don't know. His lungs're full of garbage, I'd guess. Kidneys and liver won't be too good. Have to wait. Hips might be busted. I haven't checked. He'll have a headache, that's for sure. All that time without oxygen. He's strong though.'

'Like his mother.'

The baby seemed to fill with colour before his eyes. He went a mottled yellow and pink. Jerra wanted to touch the little feet, but he contented himself with the firm grip the miniature hand had on him. So it's a reflex, he thought; what do I care.

'Will he have brain damage, you reckon?'

The man shrugged. 'I'm not God.'

He was sitting by the humidicrib when they wheeled Rachel in an hour later.

'I'm stoned,' she said.

'Pethedine,' said Annie. They'd been crying, he could tell.

'Can I hold him?'

'No,' a nurse said.

A person with a clipboard came in. 'Mrs Nilsam, you're in room six.'

'Is that a single room?' Jerra asked.

'No. I'm afraid—'

'You see, the thing is I'll need to stay with my—'

'I'm sorry, you—'

'Look, for one, we're entitled under all that blood insurance we paid, and two, because my wife's just had—'

'Mr Nilsam, I—'

'OK, I'll sleep in the corridor. I'm about to be hysterical.'

'I'll see what I can do.'

'He's alive,' Rachel said.

'Call him Samuel,' said Annie. 'I reckon you should.'

'Sam.'

'Sure,' said Jerra, shaking as though a fit had come upon him. 'He's alive, isn't he?'

They lay in the dark and tried to sleep. Jerra thought of the dead fireplaces at home. He thought of the empty little house. He turned on his folding cot and felt the huge load rise up in him and he began to weep. His body muscled up against the sobs. He tried to be quiet. Tears tracked into his hair and he tasted salt and it was as strong in his mouth as blood. Jerra Nilsam cried. He wept and did not stop and he thought his eyes would bleed, and when he found a pause in himself, he heard the big bed above him clanking. He got up and turned on a dim light. Rachel lay with a pillow between her teeth. Her eyes were breaking with tears.

'I feel so defiled,' she said.

He turned out the light and held her. She filled his arms.

In the middle of the night he crept out of the room and down the long corridor to the intensive care unit. The nurse looked at his matted hair and his bare feet. In the reflection in the glass window he saw there were bloodstains on his overalls. He went in to the lone Perspex box marked *Samuel Nilsam* and he sat down beside it. A heart monitor bleeped. It was a mournsome sound.

His son lay spreadeagled on his front with his head in an oxygen cube. His blood-caked body was bound by tubes and wires. Beneath him, his huge swollen testicles. He had black hair. He did look strong, sleeping there, sucking on a dummy; he looked strong enough to be alive.

When the charge nurse turned her back, Jerra opened the little portal at the side of the humidicrib and carefully reached in. He touched the bright pink buttocks. He ran a hand down the closest thigh and felt the textures of hair and dried blood. There was warmth there.

Footsteps.

He looked up. The nurse regarded him with indignation. Her mouth was tight. She put her hands on her hips.

Jerra Nilsam looked down and gripped an arm. His joined fingers were a bracelet on his son's wrist. He felt blood. Yes, that was blood there, and he looked up at the nurse in defiance.

'Go to hell,' he said. 'This one's mine.'